The only thing that really mattered was finding Rachel and the rest of the missing women.

Sydney's hand was already on the door handle when Tucker stopped at the gate to the Double K Ranch.

"I've got it," Tucker said. "A real cowboy never lets the bloody wounded do the work."

"More of the cowboy code?"

"If it's not, it should be."

She watched him unlatch the gate and swing it open. It was midmorning now and the sun glistened on his shirtless shoulders and chest. His muscles rippled. Bull-rider muscles, and he'd be back to that soon.

But for now he was making it clear that he was all hers. The shocker was that she was thankful to have him around.

FEARLESS GUNFIGHTER

JOANNA WAYNE

To my wonderful friend and neighbor Zona, the only former rocket scientist I can always count on to have an extra Diet Coke on hand. And in memory of her loving husband, Jim, who actually did help put a man on the moon. Also, a call-out to all my friends who love the rodeo and bull riders as much as I do. Happy reading, all.

PLEASE RECYCLE • THIS PRODUCT IS RECYCLABLE •

Recycling programs for this product may not exist in your area.

ISBN-13: 978-0-373-75698-8

Fearless Gunfighter

This edition published by arrangement with Harlequin Books S.A.

For questions and comments about the quality of this book, please contact us at CustomerService@Harlequin.com.

Printed in U.S.A.

Joanna Wayne began her professional writing career in 1994. Now, more than fifty published books later, Joanna has gained a worldwide following with her cutting-edge romantic suspense and Texas family series, such as Sons of Troy Ledger and Big "D" Dads. Joanna currently resides in a small community north of Houston, Texas, with her husband. You may write Joanna at PO Box 852, Montgomery, TX 77356, or connect with her at joannawayne.com.

Books by Joanna Wayne

Harlequin Intrigue

The Kavanaughs

Riding Shotgun
Quick-Draw Cowboy
Fearless Gunfighter

Big "D" Dads: The Daltons

Trumped Up Charges
Unrepentant Cowboy
Hard Ride to Dry Gulch
Midnight Rider
Showdown at Shadow Junction
Ambush at Dry Gulch

Sons of Troy Ledger

Cowboy Swagger
Genuine Cowboy
AK-Cowboy
Cowboy Fever
Cowboy Conspiracy

Big "D" Dads

Son of a Gun
Live Ammo
Big Shot

Visit the Author Profile page at Harlequin.com.

CAST OF CHARACTERS

Sydney Maxwell—FBI profiler, personally involved in the most important case of her career.

Tucker Lawrence—Professional bull rider faced with a decision that could change his life.

Rachel Maxwell—Sydney's sister, who's feared to be a victim of a murderous serial abductor.

Jackson Clark—Senior-level FBI and Sydney's supervisor.

Pierce and Riley Lawrence—Tucker's older brothers.

Esther Kavanaugh—Widow of Charlie Kavanaugh. The Kavanaughs took the Lawrence brothers in as teenagers when their parents died.

Dani Lawrence—Riley's wife, the owner of Dani's Delights and guardian to her niece, Constance.

Grace Lawrence—Pierce's wife and stepmother to his daughter, Jaci.

Dudley Miles—Rich rancher and best friend of Charlie Kavanaugh before Charlie's death.

Millie Miles—Dudley's wife.

Alice Baker, Michelle Dickens and Karen Murphy—Women who have recently gone missing from the Winding Creek area.

Allan Cullen, Tim Adams and Rene Foster—FBI agents on a race against time to capture the murderous serial abductor before he kills again.

Chapter One

Saturday, September 9

Rachel Maxwell opened her eyes. The world remained black. She tried to lift her arms, but blistering pain attacked with the slightest movement. She was alive. That was all she was certain of. Death couldn't hurt this bad.

Her pupils slowly adjusted to the darkness, but the hammering inside her skull was so intense her brain couldn't identify where she was or why. Random thoughts skirted her consciousness.

A faint line of brightness on the other side of the room provided the only illumination. Most likely a space beneath a door, so there must be a light on somewhere. No windows to let in a scant glow of moonlight. No sounds except her own ragged breathing.

She was on her back, stretched out, perhaps in a bed, perhaps not. Her fingers impulsively went to her face. Her cheeks felt swollen, but numb, the only part of her that didn't ache. She struggled to focus.

Fear swelled, crashing through her like ocean waves as scraps of nightmarish images crept through the shadows of her mind. The man dragging her into his truck. His creepy hands all over her.

And then the punishing blows.

Her stomach heaved as the memories grew more distinct. Not a nightmare, but horrifying reality.

She forced her body to move, slid over until her hand touched what felt like rough, splintered wood. She rolled off what must be no more than a pallet of some kind and onto the hard floor. Every joint and muscle cried out for mercy as she forced herself to scoot up on her elbows and crawl toward the light.

When she reached the door, she struggled to stand, her fingers clawing at the door frame until she could wrap them around the doorknob.

She hesitated. If the door opened, it might only lead to more hell. But the faint hint of escape held sway. She turned the knob and shoved her body against it. The door didn't budge.

She beat on the door with her fists. Agony and hopelessness took hold as she slid back to the floor. Tears filled her eyes and sobs shook her pain-racked body. She'd been imprisoned by a monster. The worst was no doubt yet to come.

Chapter Two

Tucker Lawrence braked his mud-encrusted black pickup truck in front of a small stucco-and-wood house on a quiet neighborhood street on the outskirts of Lubbock, Texas.

The home was veiled in darkness. No sounds. No sign of movement, which meant Lauren Hernandez hadn't heard the news yet. The words that would wreak havoc on her life and rip the heart from her chest.

He'd exceeded the speed limits to be the first one here, no easy feat in West Texas, where posted limits were frequently eighty miles per hour with a few stretches at eighty-five. He hadn't wanted Lauren to hear the tragic truth from a stranger.

He'd be letting Rod down if he did.

So now he'd be the one to walk up that sidewalk and ring the bell. He'd tell Lauren that the man she loved with all her heart, the father of their three young children, would never come walking through the front door again.

He wrapped his hand around the truck's door handle, but couldn't bring himself to twist it. Instead he let his head fall to the steering wheel as the heartbreaking images claimed his mind.

Six seconds into the ride on the toughest bull to come out of the chute last night. From the crack of the opening gate, Rod was doing everything right. Great technique. Terrific form. Spurring and staying in control of the bucking, twisting, spinning monster of an animal.

Two seconds to go when the bull went into a spin that threw Rod from the animal's back and drew him into the vortex. All Tucker could see from his position behind the chutes was a tangle of hooves and human body as Rod tried to free himself from impending disaster.

By the time the bull stamped off, Rod wasn't moving. He'd died two hours later from trauma to the brain.

Rod. Laughing, joking, adrenaline running

high a few hours ago. Now he was gone. All because he'd lost a battle of wills with a stupid bull acting on instinct.

It wasn't wholly about the money. Nor the glory. Nor the comradery, though all played a part in the rodeo life. It was the thrill of competition, living on the edge, facing death and never believing you wouldn't walk away, sore but breathing.

Tucker opened the door and stepped out of the truck. Dread tore at his heart anew with each clap of his boots along the cement walk. He'd do what he came for, break the news to Lauren as gently as he could.

He wouldn't even try to convince her the risk had been worth it. He wasn't sure he believed that himself now. Bull riding had lost its glory when he'd watched his friend Rod take his final breath.

But where did a man go when he walked away from the only life he knew?

Chapter Three

Monday, September 18

FBI profiler and special agent Sydney Maxwell stepped into her supervisor's office, nerves taut, geared for a fight she'd likely lose. Still, it was worth a try. If her worst fear was realized, she'd need all the inside information she could get.

Roland Farmer stood as she walked in and motioned toward the seat facing his desk. He smiled. She didn't. She liked Roland and respected his judgment, but at this moment none of that mattered to her.

Roland sat down after her, leaned back in his leather chair and tented his fingers. He stared for a few seconds before speaking as if he were trying to assess her mood.

He should have no trouble doing that. It was fear, resolve and urgency. But Roland would quickly pick up more. He'd see her determination and hear the desperation in her voice.

"Are you all right?" he asked.

She nodded. She was far from all right, but she couldn't lead off with that, not if she was to have a chance of influencing Roland to listen to reason.

"What's on your mind that's so important it couldn't wait?" he asked.

"I don't know if you're familiar with the situation, but three young women have gone missing over the past six months in the Texas Hill Country under bizarre circumstances. The body of another was found two days ago in a wooded area just outside the small town of Winding Creek."

"Winding Creek, Texas," Roland repeated. "Why does that ring a bell?"

"It was a big story on cable news for months about a year ago. A toddler fell and died from a head trauma while his mother was spaced out on heroin."

"Right," Roland said. "It's coming back to me. It wasn't our case but the mother had the whole town searching for the kid when she claimed he'd been kidnapped.

"A wealthy family, if I remember correctly. One of those ranchers whose cows scratch their backs on oil rigs. But back to the missing women. I take it you think this is a case for the FBI to look into?"

"I do. One of the missing women is from Shreveport, Louisiana, crosses state lines, so it meets our guidelines."

Roland scratched his chin. "You'll be pleased that the powers that be agree with you. It helped that the local Texas law authorities contacted the Bureau last night and requested their help. They are concerned they may have a serial killer on their hands even though only the one body has been found."

"How soon will we be sending an investigative team to the area?"

"I'd guess an assessment team will be in the field within the next forty-eight hours—maybe sooner. Jackson Clark in the Dallas field office will head up the investigation."

A tinge of relief only slightly eased her apprehension. "They'll need a profiler as well as several agents in order to move quickly."

"Are you volunteering to join Jackson's team?"

She nodded. "It makes sense. I went to school at University of Texas, UT, in Austin. I know my way around the area."

"I can put in your request with Jackson. He's aware of your success on the Swamp Strangler case. I'm sure he's impressed enough to consider you."

She'd only met Jackson Clark once when she'd attended a weeklong seminar he'd conducted in Quantico. He was a giant of a man, intimidating, demanding—a brilliant investigator. He was not known for being easily impressed.

There was no one she'd rather see handle this case.

Roland rolled his chair closer to the desk and drummed the eraser end of a pencil against a closed folder. "The only problem I see is that you seem to be taking this case personally, Sydney. If that has anything to do with the woman you couldn't save from the Swamp Strangler, you have to let that go and move on."

"It's not that." She couldn't lie. It was only a matter of time before the truth would come out and she'd risk losing her job if she didn't level with Roland. "It's even more personal," she admitted.

Roland spread his hands palms down on the table. "Keep talking."

"My sister, Rachel, is missing." The words tore at her heart and her control. She blinked back a tear and stared at the toes of her black pumps.

"I'm so sorry to hear that. Is Rachel the sister who's an attorney in Houston?"

"Yes. She's my only sister." Her only family.

"When did you find out?"

"A few minutes after nine this morning. Connie Ledger, her best friend and a coworker, called when Rachel didn't show up for work this morning and couldn't be reached by phone. Connie tried Rachel's number several times but her attempts resulted in a 'call cannot be completed' message."

Roland's brows arched. "So basically, you're saying she didn't make it into work this morning. There could be a lot of explanations for that."

"And I wouldn't be here if that were the case. Rachel took a week's vacation that started ten days ago on a Friday afternoon. Apparently, no one has heard from her since then."

Roland straightened, his chin jutting as if he was just clueing in to the fact that this was serious. "And you don't know where she was vacationing or whom she was with?"

"I know where she was supposed to be. She called me the Friday she left and said she was going to a spa resort near Austin for some R & R."

"Alone?"

"Yes, but that's not particularly unusual for Rachel. She's very independent. Her law firm had just successfully wrapped up a case that she'd worked long hours on for weeks before and during the trial. She sounded exhilarated, but exhausted."

"I assume you've contacted the resort."

"Yes. Rachel never showed up, nor did she cancel. They tried to reach her to no avail. When I call her number it just says 'party unavailable.'"

Roland pulled his lips tight across his teeth. "Is she in a relationship?"

"Not currently. She broke up with her boyfriend of four years a little over a month ago. As far as I know, she hasn't dated anyone since then."

"I'm sure you've talked to her ex."

"I called Carl this morning. So far, he hasn't called me back, but Connie reached him earlier. He wasn't aware Rachel was missing, but offered to meet Connie at Rachel's apartment to check things out."

"Did he?"

"No. Connie called the police department instead and an officer met her there. The apartment manager let them in. There was nothing amiss."

Roland leaned in close, propped his elbows and waited for Sydney to meet his scrutinizing gaze. "I know how alarming this is, but try not to jump to any frightening conclusions before you have all the facts."

"I'm not assuming anything. I'm not ruling out anything, either. Taking a vacation alone is very much like Rachel. Not returning to work on time is completely foreign to her modus operandi. She is very serious about her work. She's serious about everything."

He nodded. "Got it. You've got reason to worry. But I'll have to level with Jackson. It can get sticky working a case you're personally involved in."

"I understand, but as part of the investigation team or on my own, I have to get to Texas as soon as possible. I'm prepared to take an emergency leave if necessary and I've booked a flight to Houston that leaves here at one."

"I wouldn't expect you to do anything less." He stood and stepped around the corner of his desk. "Even if you're not officially part of the Bureau's investigation, I expect you to keep me posted. Call if there's anything we can do to help."

"Believe me, I will."

And with or without Roland's permission, she'd call on Lane Foster. Best tech geek in the business. If it was in cyberspace, he could find it. She already had a list of requests for him, some she could have done herself if she'd had the time.

Sydney stood and Roland held out his arms for a sympathetic hug that was appreciated though awkward. Roland was normally the strictly business kind of boss.

She gave a final nod, then hurried from the room, closing the door behind her. If her sister was in any kind of trouble, time was of the essence.

No one knew that better than Sydney.

Chapter Four

It was a few minutes after seven when Sydney finally made it to the front door of Rachel's condo. She'd spent most of the three hours since she'd landed renting a car, filling out a missing person's report at the downtown police precinct and being interviewed by a blunt but hopefully efficient detective. The rest of the time had been spent fighting traffic.

The detective had promised to give the case top priority though she had the distinct impression he wouldn't, at least not yet. Thankfully, she had Lane behind the scenes.

Her nerves tensed as she rummaged in her oversize travel purse for the key. Her sister had moved into the luxurious high-rise with her long-term boyfriend Carl Upton less than a year ago.

Rachel still loved the apartment but her relationship with Carl had withered and died. He'd moved out last month, and according to Rachel, they'd both moved on. He still hadn't returned her call from this morning.

Key in hand, Sydney still hesitated. It wasn't that she was afraid of what she'd find. Connie had assured her that she and the police officer had checked out every square inch of the living quarters.

It was exhaustion, fear and the dread of facing the emptiness that held Sydney back now. She forced herself to turn the key and step inside.

Sydney rolled her luggage out of the doorway and dropped her purse and her briefcase onto the small table in the entryway. The staggering sense of emptiness she'd expected didn't materialize.

Instead, the space overflowed with Rachel's aura of warmth. The scent of the many candles she'd burned whenever she was home lingered in the still air.

Everything was meticulously in order, as always. Sydney had missed out on their father's neat-freak gene but Rachel had it in spades.

Sydney walked through the living area and

into the kitchen. Nothing amiss there, either. A check of the refrigerator revealed a few jars of condiments and preserves on the door shelves and very little else.

Anything that would have spoiled while she was at the resort had obviously been tossed. The kitchen trash can was also empty. Rachel was a stickler for details. And the most reliable person Sydney knew.

She would never fail to show up for work without contacting someone.

So where was she now?

Sydney's mind searched desperately as it had all day for explanations that didn't include a conclusion too horrible to imagine. Nonetheless, the serial-killer scenario skulked through her thoughts like a dark shadow, creating a biting chill that reached to the bone.

But that was the worst-case scenario. She had to move past the crippling fear and focus on even the smallest scraps of evidence that could lead her to Rachel.

Was it possible she'd had a nervous breakdown from the pressures she'd put on herself to become the youngest partner at Fitch, Fitch and Baumer?

No. She had too much grit for that. If things

had gotten that bad, she'd have told the senior partners off and walked away from the job.

Had she been in a car crash that left her in a coma? Or perhaps had an accident that left her with temporary amnesia?

Only Sydney—with Lane's help—had checked every emergency room and hospital for miles around. No patients fit her description. And her car had not been located.

Sydney's cell phone rang. She checked the caller ID. Lane. She felt anxious and hopeful at the same time. God, did she need some good news.

"What do you have for me?" she asked as soon as they'd exchanged a quick hello.

"Rachel has used two credit cards since the last time she was seen by her coworkers."

"When, where and how much?"

"She used an American Express card on Saturday morning to pay for a room at a bed-and-breakfast in La Grange, Texas."

"Would that be on her route to Austin?"

"It would. I'll send you the rest of the details. Time, name of the B and B, address and phone number."

"Good. What else do you have?"

"She withdrew three hundred dollars cash

from an ATM a few minutes after noon that same day in the neighboring town of Winding Creek."

Winding Creek, where the body had been found. The reference rattled her nerves so badly she had to hold on to the back of the nearest chair for support.

"Do we have a photo to prove that it was actually her who withdrew the cash?"

"Working on it," Lane said.

"Were those Rachel's only charges?"

"No. She made a purchase at Dani's Delights, also in Winding Creek, for sixty-five dollars and eighty-nine cents at two eighteen."

"What kind of store is that?"

"A bakery and coffee shop."

"Rachel barely eats. She'd have never paid that much for java and scones. I don't have a map in front of me. Is Winding Creek near Austin?"

"It's south of Austin, closer to San Antonio, but not far out of her way once she left La Grange."

"What's the draw to Winding Creek? Why would she go out of her way to visit that town?"

"I don't have the answer to that."

"We know Rachel was there a little after

two on Saturday afternoon and then never made it to her scheduled destination. So somewhere between Winding Creek and the resort, Rachel's plans were ambushed."

"That's the gist of what I've found so far."

Sydney struggled to focus as the fear swelled to near suffocating. "Were you able to locate her phone?"

"Not yet. It's not putting out a signal."

It could be at the bottom of Winding Creek or perhaps hammered to smithereens like the Swamp Strangler destroyed the phones of his victims.

"Thanks for your help, Lane. At least I have a starting point."

If she left now, she could easily make it to Winding Creek tonight. If it was like most small Texas towns, the sidewalk would have already been rolled up by the time she got there, but at least she'd be there when the sun came up tomorrow morning.

Rachel could be most anywhere between here and Austin, but Winding Creek was the next stop for Sydney.

HANK'S HANGOUT WAS the only place within miles of Winding Creek that was still open at eleven thirty on Monday evening. Sydney could thank Siri for finding it.

Not that she wanted a drink or company, but it was a place to start.

She pulled into the almost-empty parking lot and got out of her car. A neon sign touted live music on the weekends and all-night happy-hour prices on Monday.

Merle Haggard's voice greeted her as she stepped inside. Faded publicity posters on the wall dated back to the era of Patsy Cline, Johnny Cash and Willie Nelson during his much-earlier years. Vintage metal plaques cautioned spurs should be removed before dancing on the bar and that horses should remain outside unless they were paying customers.

Hopefully those were in jest, though from looking at the scratched and marred surface of the bar, it had likely seen some boot scooting.

She considered staking out a bar stool, but that would have left her with her back to the rest of the room. She wasn't sure what she was looking for exactly, but anything would be better than staring at the ceiling of the motel she'd booked when sleep would be almost impossible tonight.

Taking a seat as far away from the loud music as possible, she scanned the room. To her dismay, a lot more eyes were checking her out. Not surprising since she appeared to be the only woman in there sitting alone.

Another time that kind of attention would have made her uneasy. Tonight, her mind was occupied with far more important matters.

Sydney pulled out her cell phone and punched in her instant code for Rachel the way she'd done every hour since Connie had called her that morning. The phone rang only once before a new message started.

"The number of the party you're calling is no longer in service."

She fought back yet another wave of nauseating dread as a young waitress with half-exposed breasts and a pair of butt-hugging denim cutoffs stopped at her table. Her name tag read Betts.

Betts smiled. "The kitchen's closed for the night but the bar is serving until one. What can I get you?"

"A beer, something light." That she probably wouldn't take more than a few sips of.

"I have a good craft beer on tap that would fit that description. Want to give that a try?"

"Sure."

"You've got it. Will someone be joining you?"

Sydney shook her head and went back to scrutinizing the customers. A half dozen or so couples were two-stepping around the dance floor. A few more couples occupied tables, chatting and sipping drinks.

For most, dress was casual, jeans or shorts. Footwear was predominantly Western boots for the men and sandals for the women. No one stood out as suspicious, except for Sydney in her black slacks and tailored white shirt.

A cute cowboy in faded jeans with a nice smile ambled over to her table. "Mind if I join you and buy you a drink?"

"Sorry, but no. I was supposed to meet a friend but I think she may have already left." Sydney unzipped her purse, reached into the side pocket and pulled out a recent photo of Rachel.

She handed it to the cowboy. "Have you seen her?"

He glanced at the photo. "No, but she's a looker. I'm sure I'd remember if I'd ever seen her and I'm in here often."

He stepped back and stared critically. "You're not a cop or something, are you?"

FBI no doubt qualified as his *or something*, but she wasn't ready to reveal that to anyone in Winding Creek just yet.

"I'm not a cop."

He placed the picture on the table. "If you get bored and change your mind about wanting some company tonight, you know where to find me. I guarantee you a good time."

"I'll keep that in mind."

Betts returned with a cold mug of beer and set it and a throwaway coaster on the table next to the picture. She didn't give the photo a second glance.

Sydney decided her questions for Betts could wait. A few customers had left in the short time she'd been here. Time now would be best spent checking out the remaining customers.

Not that she held out any rational hope of just accidentally running into someone who was involved in Rachel's disappearance. Irrationally, she couldn't help but search for someone who triggered suspicion or a situation that piqued her interest.

Fifteen minutes later, she got her wish. She

was watching the door when a tall cowboy who looked as if he'd been living on the streets sauntered into the bar. Tall, lean but muscular and with at least two days' growth of whiskers.

Unlike the other customers who seemed to know everyone, he didn't speak to or acknowledge any of the patrons as he walked past the bar and dropped into a chair several tables away from her.

He removed his white Western hat and ran his fingers through short, rumpled brown hair. Betts sashayed over and leaned in so close her nipples were practically looking him in the eye.

He seemed not to notice.

Sydney couldn't hear what he ordered, but Betts returned a minute later with what looked like a glass of whiskey. It was gone in two gulps.

She was still staring at him when he lifted his gaze and looked in her direction. His eyes were mesmerizing even from that distance, bronze colored in the artificial light.

She looked away and tried to make sense of what she was feeling. Her profiler instincts and training checked in. Something about him was affecting her senses. She couldn't just ignore that.

Sydney motioned to Betts.

"Ready for another beer?"

"Haven't started this one yet. I just have a question for you."

"Yeah. What?"

"See the guy sitting at the table by himself?" She nodded toward him.

"Yeah. Quite a hunk, isn't he, but not too friendly."

"So it appears. Is he a regular?"

"Nope. If he was I'd remember him, though he does look a little familiar."

"Are you sure he wasn't in here Saturday night before last?"

"Can't say. I was off that weekend. Went to my sister's wedding over in New Braunfels. I don't think he's local, though. More likely he's renting one of the fishing cabins up near the marina. Looks like a guy on a fishing vacation."

"Are there that many fish to be had from a creek?"

"Oh, yeah, and if you don't want to fish in the creek, there are lakes all around here. They have big fishing rodeos every year in the spring. Man, do we get the fishermen in here then. Tips are great."

"Just one more thing," Sydney said. She picked up the photo of Rachel and handed it to Betts. "Have you ever seen this woman before? She's about five foot six, slender, thirty-two years old?"

Betts studied the photo for a few seconds and then looked back at Sydney. "Nope. Why?"

"She's an old friend of mine who moved to this area a few years ago. I thought I'd look her up while I'm visiting the area, but I'm not sure where she lives."

"Try social media. You can find most everybody on there, even people you don't want to find."

"I'll keep that in mind."

There were fewer couples on the dance floor now and a lot more empty seats at the bar. Evidently the party ended early on Monday evenings. Sydney sipped her beer, stood and walked over to the stranger's table before he decided to cut out, as well.

"Mind if I join you?" she asked, trying for a flirty voice but likely falling short.

"You can sit. It's a waste of time. Whatever you're looking for, you're not going to find it in me."

"What if it's a good time?"

"Then you really need to look elsewhere."

"What if it's only conversation?"

"You can do better talking to yourself."

"You are scraping the bottom of the blues," she said. "Do you live in Winding Creek?"

"Nope."

"Me, either. Where do you live?"

"Wherever I kick off my boots."

Her suspicions surged. "Do you have a name, cowboy?"

"Why do you want to know?"

"If we find ourselves kicking off our boots in the same town one night, I might want to look you up."

"It's Tucker. Tucker Lawrence. But don't bother to look me up. I got nothing going on. Absolutely nothing." He pulled a ten-dollar bill from his wallet and stuck one end of it under his empty glass. "Enjoy your visit to Winding Creek."

Tucker stood, picked up his hat, tipped it and strode out of the bar the way he'd come in, looking straight ahead and not saying a word to anyone.

Sydney walked back to her table, left money for her tab and tip, and then followed Tucker Lawrence out the door. He was already in his truck and pulling away when she jumped into her car and followed him. He might not live in Winding Creek, but if not, he must be staying somewhere nearby.

There was probably at least a 99 percent chance that he was a dead end, but there was always that 1 percent. At least she'd know how to find him again if she needed to and she knew his name unless he'd lied about it.

Sydney followed Tucker down the highway a few miles before turning onto a dark country back road. He took the unfamiliar curves without lowering his speed, making it difficult for her to keep up.

He turned off onto another road, more narrow, hilly and winding than the first. She was almost up with him when she spotted the deer in her peripheral vision.

She threw on her brakes and skidded to a stop just as the animal darted onto the blacktop road. Her heart jumped from her chest at the soft thumping and the jerky movement as the car rolled to a full stop.

She sprang out of the car not thinking that a

wounded animal could be dangerous until she got closer to the large buck. The stunned animal stared into her headlights accusingly for a few seconds and then raced to the other side of the road and disappeared into the woods.

No limp. No signs of significant injury. Relief rolled through her. She checked out her car. There were a few stray hairs in her left bumper, but not even a dent. Luckily, she'd seen the deer in time to prevent real damage to it or her or the rental car. She climbed back behind the wheel. Tucker Lawrence was long gone.

By the time Sydney got back to Hank's to question the owner himself, he was gone, as well. Reportedly left early on what he considered a slow night.

There was nothing left for her to do but go check into her motel room and try to get some sleep. Only how could she close her eyes not knowing what Rachel might be facing tonight?

Already missing ten days. The urgency burned like fire deep in Sydney's soul.

THE WOMAN IN Hank's had told it like it was. A man was in damn bad shape when he couldn't shake the blues enough to respond to a stunning woman who'd made the first move.

Tucker had moped around for almost a week, spending most of that time in cheap motels between here and Lubbock though he could have afforded first class.

The cheap motels had seemed a better match for his lower-than-a-snake's-belly mood. He'd stayed in Lubbock just long enough for Lauren's parents to make the flight from Baton Rouge, Louisiana, to Lubbock to be with their devastated daughter.

Lauren had taken the news of Rod's death as badly or worse than Tucker had expected. At one point, Tucker had to literally hold her up to keep her from hitting the floor. Only thing that held her even halfway together until her parents arrived was that the kids needed her.

She was a train wreck, shock and heartbreak reducing her to a state of helplessness that mimicked that of her toddler daughter.

Tucker hadn't been in a lot better shape himself, but watching Lauren face the tragedy rode his nerves even harder.

Living, breathing, laughing one minute. Brain-dead six seconds later, though Rod's body had managed to hold on to life for two more hours.

All for what? That was the question that wouldn't let go of Tucker.

He should be in Oklahoma this coming weekend, competing in one of the best-paying rodeos in the September circuit. He'd started in that direction twice, had even made it to the outskirts of Tulsa once, only to turn around and head back to Texas.

His life was bull riding. It was all he'd ever known. All he wanted to know. But that could have just as easily been his skull the bull was stamping instead of Rod's.

Had watching Rod struggle for that last breath turned Tucker into a coward? Or was he finally developing some brains to go with the testosterone that usually fueled him?

He stopped in front of the gate to the Double K Ranch and left his engine running while he got out, pulled the latch and sent the gate swinging wide.

A few minutes later, he stopped a few yards down from the front of Esther Kavanaugh's sprawling ranch house. He felt years older than he had a couple of months ago when he was here for his brother Riley's wedding.

The house looked the same as it had the first time he'd wound up at Esther's door almost as done in as he felt now. That time it had been his parents who had died unexpectedly.

He started to get out of the truck but reconsidered when he realized there wasn't a light on in the house. Ranchers rose at sunrise. No use to wake everyone in the house this late.

They'd have questions. He was in no mood to answer them tonight. Morning would be soon enough to lay his problems on his two older brothers and Esther.

If anyone could help him come to grips with his twisted emotions, it would be Pierce and Riley. If anyone could figuratively give him a kick in the rear that would get him going again, it would be Esther Kavanaugh.

Come to think of it, the kick might be more than figurative if she felt like he needed it.

He shoved his seat back as far as it would go, stretched his legs out beneath the dashboard and made himself as comfortable as he could.

Fatigue set in. His eyes grew heavy. His mind took a crazy turn. He fell asleep wondering what the woman from Hank's would have felt like in his arms if he'd asked her to dance.

Tuesday, September 19:

RACHEL SAT HUNCHED in the corner like a guilty child in time-out. The room was still dark but her eyes had adjusted enough to the scant strip of light pushing in from beneath the door that she could make her way around the shadowy environment. Additional light would have made the cramped space even more miserable.

She'd lost count of the days she'd been here. They ran together like drops of spilled coffee. The strong, black brew was delivered every morning, usually accompanied with dry, cold and frequently burned toast.

That was her only way of knowing that a new day had started. The coffee was the bright spot in the vacuous existence devoid of everything except dread and visions of escape.

As much as she craved the coffee, she never finished the full cup. Show that she enjoyed something too much and the monster would stop bringing it.

She never knew what to expect from his visits. Vile language. Threats. Painful slaps to her face or shoves that sent her crashing to the floor.

Bizarrely, there were also times that he showed a hint of compassion. Like the second time he'd visited her in this hellhole.

She'd been starving. He'd come with a bowl of what tasted like chicken stock. Her pain had been so intense, her joints and muscles so swollen and inflamed she couldn't get the spoon to her mouth.

He'd fed her, slowly, encouraging her to swallow. When she'd had her fill, he wiped her face with a wet cloth and pushed several pills into her mouth. For the pain, he'd said. She didn't trust him, but she swallowed them anyway.

She'd fallen asleep almost instantly. When she woke, the thin sheets on the pallet that were stained with her blood had been changed and her laundered clothes were thrown over the one uncomfortable straight-back chair in the room.

There was also a small heavily stained sink and commode in the back corner, separated from the rest of the space by a dirty strip of printed cotton held by nails in the ceiling.

Who'd have ever believed she'd be thrilled for filthy facilities like that? Hot tears pushed at the backs of her eyelids. Would she ever escape the monster?

The sound of a slamming door cracked through the silence. Rachel's pulse pounded. Her body trembled.

He was coming.

She hunched farther back in the corner, hugging her arms around her knees. The doorknob turned. The door squeaked open. The pungent odor of garlic and sweat swept into the room with the monster.

She studied his face before the door closed behind him, shutting out the extra light. He smiled as he always did, a big grin that told her just how much he was enjoying this.

He set a tray of food on the floor. "Did you miss me?" His tone was cocky and teasing, as if they were friends or lovers. Her skin crawled at the thought, though blessedly he hadn't touched her sexually—yet.

"Why are you doing this?" she asked. "Why are you keeping me here?"

"I hate coming home to an empty house after a hard day at work." He chuckled at his sick joke.

"I have money," Rachel said. "A lot of

money. I can pay you whatever you want if you'll just let me go free."

"If I gave you your freedom, I'd lose mine. Besides, I already have a woman who gives me all the money I ask for."

"I can give you more. I won't go to the police. I promise. I'll stay out of your life forever and never mention this to anyone."

He chuckled again. "Now, why would I let you go now? Your ugly bruises are almost gone. It no longer makes me sick to look at you."

"You'll never get away with this."

"That's where you're wrong, sweet lady. People get away with far worse all the time. No one cares what you do as long as it doesn't affect them. Even murder gets buried in the haystack."

Eventually he'd kill her, but he'd do it slow and torturously, get his rocks off on her fear, revel in her misery as if it were a sexual adventure.

How sick would a man have to be to do that?

If Sydney were here, she'd be able to figure him out. She'd get in his mind, discover the demons that drove him. She'd find his weaknesses and use them against him.

Sydney wasn't here, but she'd know by now that Rachel hadn't come home from her vacation. She'd be certain something was terribly wrong.

She'd found the Swamp Strangler when no one else could. She'd find Cowboy Monster, too.

All Rachel had to do was stay alive and sane until she did.

Chapter Five

Esther Kavanaugh stretched and kicked off the lightweight blanket. The oppressive summer heat and humidity hadn't given in to autumn yet. It seldom did in September, but she had no complaints.

The new cooling and heating system Pierce had installed kept the house as cool and comfortable as she wanted it no matter what the temperature outside. He'd made a dozen other repairs on the old house, as well.

His brother Riley pitched in and helped, even though he was newly married as well and establishing his own ranch right down the road.

That was the kind of young men the Lawrence brothers had grown into. She was thankful for them every day and had loved all three of them since the day she first met them. Now they were literally giving her a reason to keep breathing and getting up every morning to face a new day.

Pierce had been the first to come to her rescue after her husband's death. He'd shown up one morning with his adorable five-year-old daughter, Jaci, just in the nick of time, as the saying went.

Since she was no longer able to pay her bills or take care of the Double K Ranch, he'd offered to buy the ranch from her—house, barns, livestock and all, closed on it days before foreclosure officers at the bank got a chance to get their greedy hands on everything she and Charlie had struggled all those years to build.

Selling the ranch to Pierce wasn't even like losing it. She'd likely have willed it to him anyway since he was the oldest of the brothers she considered her only family.

She'd sold it to Pierce for the price it took to keep it out of foreclosure so he could use the rest of his savings to get the ranch running efficiently again.

She hadn't asked him for a thing in return, but he'd made her a verbal promise that she'd have her house, her garden and her chickens until the day the good Lord called her home.

No reason for a paper contract when you dealt with a man who was as good as his word.

Best part of all was now she had Pierce, his wife, Grace, and Jaci making their home at the ranch. They'd moved into their own cabin two weeks ago, but they were close enough they were in and out of her house every day. And she had Riley, his wife, Dani, and her niece Constance living only a few miles away.

That only left their younger brother, Tucker, for her to worry about.

A world-class bull rider who thrived on the danger and excitement of rodeo life. Followed the circuit, constantly on the move. How was he ever going to meet the right woman when all he had time for was those buckle bunnies out looking for a good time?

He thought he was living the good life but he kept Esther busy just praying he didn't get hurt by one of those kicking, stamping, snorting bulls.

Worries or not, taking in the Lawrence brothers had been one of the smartest things she and Charlie had ever done.

Instinctively her hand reached over and

touched the spot where her husband had slept beside her for most of her adult life. The familiar ache grew heavy in her chest. Lord knew she missed that man. Always would.

But lying here getting all pitiful over things she couldn't change wouldn't bring Charlie back. She threw her legs over the side of the bed and wiggled her feet into her slippers before padding to the kitchen.

By the time the coffee was ready, the sun had topped the horizon and the roosters were crowing their welcome to a new day. She filled her favorite mug with the brew, the cup Pierce's daughter, Jaci, had given her that said I "heart" Grandma.

That little girl could sure make Esther's heart smile.

Esther spooned a smidgen of sugar into her coffee. She'd have liked a heaping teaspoonful but Doc Carter kept harping on her to take it easy on her sweets.

Of course, if she listened to everything that old pill pusher said, she might as well be eating cowhide and clover.

Pierce and Riley would be up and hard at work by now—rancher's hours. But one or both would be stopping by later knowing she'd have a hearty breakfast waiting. She'd been cooking big ranch breakfasts for more than half a century and she'd be doing it as long as she was able.

Coffee in hand, she walked through the family room to the front door. Nothing like swaying in her new porch swing and sharing the first light of day with the early birds who'd be flitting around her feeders instead of out searching for worms.

She turned the key in the door only to re-alize she'd forgotten to lock it again. Years of habit were hard to break although Pierce cautioned her times were changing. They just changed a lot slower around the town of Winding Creek than they did in the big cities.

She opened the door and stepped outside.

"What the dickens?"

She stared at a mud-encrusted truck parked rock-throwing distance from her house. She was about to go get her shotgun and check it out when she saw a hairy-faced man step out of the truck and stretch like he was trying to get the kinks out of his muscles.

Oh m'God. It was Tucker. She set her mug on the porch railing post and raced to greet him.

He opened his arms and she threw herself into them.

"Sorry if I smell as disgusting as I feel," he said.

She stood back and took a gander at him. "You look like you've been sleeping with the cows. How long have you been in that truck?"

"A day or two."

"Without sleep. That's dangerous, Tucker. You could..."

He slipped an arm around her ample waist. "Calm down. I got plenty of sleep, just not in a bed. Lights were all out when I got here and I didn't want to wake up the whole household."

"There's no one here to wake up but me."

"Where's Pierce and his crew?"

"They moved into their own cabin two weeks ago."

"That was fast. All he had was a foundation and a shell when I was here for Riley's wedding. I figured it would be Thanksgiving before he had it livable."

"He had lots of help from Riley and the neighbors, which you'd know if you came around more often. I can't believe your brothers didn't tell me you were coming today."

"They don't know. It was a spur-of-the-moment decision. I had a few days off before I hit the next rodeo and decided to stop by for one of your famous breakfasts. Fresh yard eggs, thick slices of bacon, fluffy biscuits and homemade blackberry jam. My mouth's already watering."

"You came to the right place. First thing you need is to find a razor and I 'spect a shower wouldn't hurt none, either."

He rubbed his heavily whiskered chin. "Right on both counts." He reached back in the truck for a duffel and slung it over his shoulder.

Just having him here lit up her world, but she wasn't quite buying the spur-of-the-moment excuse. Something was bothering him. He was saying the right things, but the words didn't quite ring true. It wasn't just his haggard appearance. She could see trouble in his eyes and hear it in his voice.

She'd pry the truth out of him later. Right now she was going to do what would make them both feel good.

Feed him.

TUCKER KICKED OUT of his boots, stripped out of his clothes and stepped into the shower.

Pipes creaked in the old house, but the water was hot and his cramped muscles reveled in the massaging spray.

Crazy that this place had the feel of home though he'd only lived in it for ten months. Painful months of grieving and coming to grips with an existence that would never again include his parents.

He'd been afraid, angry and, most of all, heartbroken. The Kavanaughs had helped him make it through the trauma, especially Esther. Her faith, love and compassion had been his salvation.

He didn't expect that kind of miracle this time. The answers he needed now had to come from inside himself.

By the time he'd showered, shaved and dressed in a pair of his most worn and comfortable jeans, the odors of bacon and coffee were doing a number on his stomach.

He shoved his feet into his boots and started down the hall. Laughter and familiar voices chimed in before he reached the kitchen. Esther had clearly wasted no time in spreading the news that he was here.

"What are you two freeloaders doing here?" he joked as he joined his brothers in the kitchen.

"Checking to see why you came sneaking in like a horse thief in the middle of the night," Pierce said.

"I just figured you stopped by to rub in how much money you're making working eight seconds a night," Riley said, pulling him into a playful neck hold.

"No way. I just came by for Esther's cooking."

"I can buy that," Pierce said. "Let's get to it before the biscuits get cold."

Breakfast turned into a boisterous, laid-back reunion. He needed that more than either of them would guess.

SYDNEY STARED INTO the bathroom mirror, her reflection a haunting image of the agony that had kept her awake most of the night. Her eyelids were puffy, the circles below her eyes dark.

The little sleep she'd gotten had been restless and interrupted by frightening nightmares where Rachel was crying for help or fighting for her life.

The highway noises hadn't helped. Eighteen-wheelers sounded as if they were roaring through her room. Exhaustion would work against her. She needed to be fully alert today, picking up on every clue no matter how small or how well hidden.

She knew from experience and training that it was the seemingly unimportant details that frequently made the difference.

Her sister had spent almost seventy dollars in a bakery. That couldn't have all been for coffee and sweets, but it was a large enough purchase that hopefully whoever had waited on Rachel would remember her. They might recall if she'd been alone or with someone. If she'd seemed distraught or worried. If anyone had harassed her in any way.

Reaching for her brush, Sydney ran it through her layered sandy-blond hair, attempting to force the unruly locks into place. She was only mildly successful.

Her movements on automatic, Sydney applied the basics—moisturizing sunscreen, eyeliner, mascara, a smear of gloss on her lips. The first stop of the morning would be Dani's Delights.

Her phone rang on her way to her car. She fished it from her handbag and checked the caller ID. FBI.

Was it possible Jackson Clark wanted her on the case despite her personal connection?

Her surge of optimism was quickly followed by a sharp pain to her stomach that almost doubled her over.

Please don't let this be bad news about Rachel, she prayed silently as she took the call.

"Is this Agent Sydney Maxwell?"

"Yes."

"Can you hold for a minute? Jackson Clark in the Dallas office of the Bureau would like to speak to you."

"Yes."

She held her breath the few seconds before his booming voice came through. "Thanks for holding, Sydney."

"No problem." No hint in his tone that this was a bad-news call. She breathed easier.

"I don't think we've met but I'm familiar with your work," Jackson said, "especially that amazing job you did on the Swamp Strangler case."

"Thank you. We haven't officially met," she agreed, "but I took one of your classes at Quantico."

"Sorry I don't remember. Those classes are

usually overflowing and I'm busy trying to cover more than the time allows."

"I didn't expect you to remember me."

"I hope I didn't call you at a bad time," he said, "but I just got off the phone with Roland Farmer. He mentioned your sister didn't show up at a resort near Austin a little over a week ago and hasn't been heard from since. I hope you have good news by now."

"No, sir. She's still missing and I'm extremely concerned." Panic verging on hysteria would be more accurate, but a good FBI agent never admitted panic.

"I'm really sorry to hear that," Jackson said. "I'm sure you've talked to local law enforcement."

"Yes, and checked all the hospitals as well as ran a paper trail. The last place we have any record of her whereabouts was a charge she'd made to a credit card in a bakery in Winding Creek, Texas, called Dani's Delights."

"Yes. I also have that information. Does she have relatives or friends in that area?"

"No relatives for certain and no friends that I know of."

"How much do you know about the other

women who have gone missing from that area over the past six months?"

"Just the facts that are publicly available. Names. Dates of disappearance. Descriptions. That sort of thing."

"But you think Rachel could be the fourth victim of the perp or perhaps fifth if he killed the girl whose body was found Saturday."

"I think it's possible. Her disappearance fits the pattern. In any case, I think she's met with foul play and is in immediate danger."

"Based on what I've heard, I think you could be right. Bottom line, I'm heading up a team of agents to help the locals investigate."

"When will you start?"

"Is today soon enough for you?"

"Yes. We need to act fast before another body shows up. All of the women are likely in extreme danger."

"I don't know if you've heard but the body has been identified as Sara Goodwin, a sixteen-year-old runaway who was apparently living on the streets in San Antonio. She was never reported as missing, so we have little information on her except what we have from forensics."

"Which is?"

"Preliminary indications are that she was dead for up to a month before they found the body. Cause of death is believed to be by trauma to the head caused by a sharp object."

"Did they find any DNA or other evidence to help identify the perp?"

"Nothing firm at this point. The reason I called is that Roland said you were willing to be assigned to this case."

"More than willing." She needed all the information the FBI could uncover to help her find Rachel.

"In that case, welcome aboard. How soon can you get to Winding Creek, Texas?"

"I'm already here, on my way to Dani's Delights."

"Perfect."

"Then you're not worried about my extremely close relationship with one of the victims?"

"I don't give a damn about protocol when lives are involved. You're a gifted profiler. You proved that on the Swamp Strangler case."

"Thank you."

"I'm leaving my office in about thirty minutes and heading your way. I'll be meeting with Sheriff Cavazos when I get there, but after that I'd like you and the other agents to be available for a full briefing. I'll call you when I have the meeting place verified."

Off and running. She liked Jackson Clark better by the second.

"One other thing," he said. "Don't identify yourself as an FBI agent or as Rachel's sister just yet. I may want you to go undercover on this unless you've already blown that option."

"I showed Rachel's picture to a cowboy and a waitress at a local roadhouse last night and asked if they'd seen her. Neither had. I didn't mention that she was my sister or even that she was missing."

"Can't undo that. If it comes out, so be it, but don't mention Rachel again. Get out there, look over the town and the area, talk to people while we're gathering as much information as we can on the missing girls. You've got a talent for noting what most people miss. Use it."

"I'll need an identity."

"In the works. Lane will be forwarding you a driver's license and establishing the background materials. You're Syd Cotton, a freelance travel/photographer from New York. It's your first time to this area of Texas, so naturally you'll be asking lots of questions and nosing around."

"I'll stick to that until you tell me differently."

"I'll be in touch around noon and, Sydney, glad to have you aboard. I think you'll be a real asset to our team."

As excited as she was to be on the insider team, the thought of working undercover made her uncomfortable. She'd planned to question the staff in the bakery, see what they remembered about Rachel.

Now the best she could do was look around. She didn't see how much could come of that. It was difficult to imagine a madman choosing his victims as they enjoyed their morning scones and coffee.

But then, stranger things had happened.

THE TOWN OF Winding Creek was like a movie set re-creation of the Old West. The low wooden buildings had surely been standing since gambler brawls and gunslingers overflowed from the bars and into the narrow streets.

Only now the stores sold fragrant candles, silver Christmas ornaments, sequined Western shirts and stylish cowboy boots. Main Street, with its brightly painted benches, pots filled with flowers in full bloom and even a few hitching posts along the curb, was so quaint it almost seemed a facade.

A horse trailer pulled by an oversize black pickup truck squeaked to a stop at a traffic light.

Two elderly gentlemen in denim coveralls slouched on one of the benches, their Western hats pulled low over their foreheads to block the sun. Crumbs from the giant cinnamon rolls they were devouring fell from their mouths to the front of their shirts.

Even more intriguing were the smiles and nods and the tipping of straw Stetsons from strangers. It was easy to see why Rachel had felt it worthwhile to take a side trip to Winding Creek. It was far more difficult to imagine evil lurking among the smiles and welcoming shops.

But somewhere between the bakery and the resort, something had gone terribly wrong. Sydney picked up her pace and hastened the last half block to the bakery.

Her pulse quickened as she stepped inside Dani's Delights. She was struck immediately by the shop's mouthwatering odors and glass cases filled with tempting pastries. The attractive redhead behind the counter was pouring coffee into tall white mugs as she chatted and laughed with her customers.

Sydney sidestepped the line of about a half dozen people waiting for service. The morning rush hour was apparently in full swing with at least half the square metal tables occupied. The noise level was high as the occupants communicated with not only the friends at their table but those sitting several tables away.

The small-town atmosphere registered solidly in Sydney's mind. There seemed to be few strangers in the group, but then, this was half past eight on a weekday morning. The clientele might be vastly different on a Saturday afternoon when Rachel had been here.

Sydney scanned the space. Blue painted shelves filled with inexpensive gift items lined the left wall. A display of unique pottery pieces filled eye-catching mahogany shelves near a back staircase.

Sydney was immediately drawn to the vases, pitchers and bowls in the pottery area, as she was certain her sister would have been.

Sydney picked up and checked the price on the bottom of a small but striking vase glazed in the earthy colors Rachel loved.

Ninety-five dollars. More than the amount Rachel had charged. Sydney checked additional items. There were several bowls and pots in the sixty-to seventy-dollar price range.

"They're made by a local artist."

The voice startled Sydney. She spun around and found herself looking into the expressive eyes of the redhead who'd been serving coffee. A quick glance back at the counter revealed that there was no longer a line.

"The potter does beautiful work," Sydney responded. "I have a sister who'd love the colors and designs."

"You should bring her in or take her to visit the artist's studio. She has a lot more choices than I can display. I can give you her card if you're interested."

"Yes, please do."

"Do you live around here?"

Sydney took a few seconds to compose a response that Jackson would approve. "I live in New York but I'm certainly enjoying your charming town."

"Do you have family in Winding Creek?"

"No. Actually I'm here for work."

"Now you've piqued my curiosity. What kind of work brings you to our small town?"

"I'm a freelancer. I do travel articles for a variety of magazines and newspapers. I'm thinking this one will feature Winding Creek but include the surrounding area and some interesting anecdotes about the inhabitants."

"You'll meet no shortage of interesting people, that's for sure. Where are you staying?"

"I'm at the motel for now but I hope to find something a little roomier and with some atmosphere."

"There are several popular B and Bs in town that would fit that description."

The bell over the front door dinged as a couple of middle-aged women walked in.

"Best get back to my duties, but if you'll stop by the counter before you go, I'll give you the addresses for the B and Bs and the pottery studio."

"Thanks. I'd appreciate that. And, of course, I want to try your coffee and a pastry before I go."

"Good. I hope you become a regular while you're here."

"I'm sure I will. Do you work every day?"

"Except on rare occasions. I'm Dani, the owner and creator of all the delights. Well, except for the bread. My hubby is fast taking over in that department."

"Sounds like a keeper."

"He definitely is."

Sydney took another look around the shop and then walked to the counter and got in line behind a woman who was choosing an assortment of cupcakes. The bell over the door dinged again and this time it was two extremely good-looking cowboys who sauntered in.

Brothers, she'd bet from their strong resemblance. One looked a bit familiar. She stared until she realized why.

He was the suspicious stranger she'd tried to follow when he'd left the bar last night.

He looked different all cleaned up, but there wasn't a doubt in her mind that it was the same man. He'd made a point of ignoring her attempts at conversation last night. He might not be that dismissive and rude since he wasn't alone.

She went for her most seductive smile and looked him in the eye as he approached the counter.

"Remember me, Tucker Lawrence?"

Chapter Six

Tucker stared for a second before nodding. "You're the woman from Hank's."

"That's right. Fancy running into you again."

"Wait, you two know each other?" the other cowboy asked.

"We exchanged howdys at Hank's last night."

"That explains why you got to the ranch so late you had to sleep in your truck."

Dani finished serving the customer and stepped from behind the counter.

"Tucker Lawrence. It's about time you paid us poor working relatives a visit." She went in for a hug before turning to Sydney. "Did I just hear that you've already met my amazing brother-in-law?"

"We ran into each other like Tucker said,

except that I'm pretty sure *howdy* never came out of my mouth."

Dani laughed. "In that case, we need some real introductions before the next paying customers walk through the door."

She took Riley's arm. "This is my husband, Riley Lawrence, and his brother Tucker."

"And I'm..." Sydney hesitated, but only for a second. "I'm Syd Cotton."

"She's a freelance writer working on an article about our town. Why don't you three find a seat and I'll pour us some coffee," Dani offered.

"I never turn down coffee," Sydney said, "but I don't want to intrude on your family time."

"There will be interruptions whether you're sitting with us or not. Not that I'm complaining. No customers, no income with which to pay the bills.

"Since the guys just had breakfast at Esther's I know they can't hold another bite of food, but can I get you something to eat, Syd? Perhaps a bacon-and-egg croissant."

"They're to die for," Riley said. "You can take my word for it. I sleep with the cook."

Sydney wasn't hungry, but she needed

something in her stomach or she'd risk a blistering headache by the time she met with Jackson.

"Sounds wonderful," Sydney agreed.

"I'll get the coffees and the croissant," Riley volunteered. "You two see if you can talk Tucker into staying a few days. I've got a horse barn that needs a roof, so might as well put those muscles of his to work doing something useful."

"My muscles are on break," Tucker quipped, "but my supervisory skills are available to the highest bidder."

"I'm married now," Riley said playfully. "I get supervisory services for free."

"Only when you need them," Dani chimed in as he walked away.

Tucker held their chairs while she and Dani settled into them. Once they were seated Dani reached over and touched Tucker's arm.

"You certainly generated some excitement this morning, showing up without anyone knowing you were coming. Esther was so delighted when she called to tell us, she could barely talk straight."

"Esther gets excited easily."

"She does," Dani agreed. "She's such a

dear. If you have time while you're here, I'd like you to meet her, Syd. She's in her early seventies, but she's the quintessential Texas rancher's wife. Good-hearted, hard worker, and she'd do anything for you."

"I'd love to meet her."

"You know, Esther might be willing to rent you a room or two for a few days. She lives in a huge rambling house just a few miles from town on the Double K Ranch. You'd even have Tucker to show you around the ranch and give you an introduction to that lifestyle from an insider's vantage point."

"I'll be leaving tomorrow," Tucker said, putting an end to that possibility before Sydney had a chance to answer.

"Why so soon?" Dani questioned. "You just got here."

"I have obligations elsewhere."

"Esther will be crushed and Riley will be disappointed. I know he wants to personally introduce you to every new Black Angus he's purchased to start his new herd."

"That's next on today's agenda," Tucker said. "We just drove into town to deliver some supplies he picked up for you."

"I know. He's wonderful, isn't he?"

"If you say so." Tucker stretched his long legs beneath the table.

Riley showed up with a tray of coffees and the croissant just as two middle-aged women with elaborately coiffed hair reminiscent of several decades past entered the shop.

"The Simmons sisters," Dani said. "Two caramel lattes, one with whipped cream, one without, and one chocolate-filled croissant, cut in half and placed on two saucers."

"I'll take care of them," Riley said. "Eleanor Simmons has a secret crush on me. Might as well make her day."

Dani rubbed his back. "Well, who wouldn't have a crush on you, sweetie? But I know exactly how much whipped cream she likes on her coffee, so I'll give you a hand."

They walked away, leaving Sydney and Tucker alone at the small table. A purposeful move, Sydney suspected, since for some strange reason Dani appeared to be playing matchmaker.

The feisty pastry chef would change her mind quickly about that if she realized everything Sydney had just said about herself was a lie.

Sydney sipped her coffee and considered

where she should take the conversation. Sitting here in silence was getting her nowhere, but blurting out leading questions would blow her cover before she even got started.

"Did you grow up around here?" she asked.

"Lived here for the first thirteen years of my life."

"Where did you live after that?"

"Kansas."

"Do you still have family here, other than your brother, I mean?"

"I have two brothers, Pierce and Riley. They both live around here. They're the only family I've got."

"Then you're not kin to the woman Dani refers to as Esther?"

"Do you always ask so many questions?"

"I'm just basically a very curious person."

"Sorry. I'm not basically a grouch. I just have a lot on my mind. It doesn't excuse my behavior. No use taking my troubles out on you."

"Apology accepted."

She decided on a different approach. "Life in a close-knit community like Winding Creek is a novel experience for me. It seems like such a safe, friendly area."

"It is."

"But I heard on the news that three women are missing from this area of Texas."

"You got me there. I'm not good about keeping up with the news."

"Not even on social media?"

"Especially not on social media. Cowboys are men of action. We do not chat, eat quiche or drink green smoothies. That's your Texas facts of the day."

"I'll be sure it makes my journal."

By the time the Simmonses had their lattes, there were another four people in line. Dani was on the phone. Riley was bagging pastries.

Sydney and Tucker stayed silent until both Riley and Dani rejoined them.

Dani shot Riley a conspiratorial look. "I just got off the phone with Esther Kavanaugh. I told her about you needing a place to stay for a few days and she said she'd love to have you as long as you didn't expect anything fancy."

"She hasn't even met me," Sydney said.

"I have, and she knows I'm a great judge of character. Besides, the people at a B and B would never have met you, either."

"It's a tempting offer," Sydney admitted. Exactly what she needed—an opportunity to start insinuating herself into the entwinements of the community. "I'll need to see the place before I make a decision."

"Naturally," Dani said. "Riley and Tucker can drive you out there now. You can see the house and the ranch and Esther will have a chance to meet you."

"I thought Tucker was supposed to be saying 'howdy' to a pasture full of black cows," Sydney said.

"We'll still have time for that," Riley assured her.

"I can't be gone long," Sydney said without giving the reason why.

"You won't have to. Riley will drive you back to town whenever you're ready."

Tucker didn't say a word but he did not look pleased.

Sydney turned back to Dani. "Just one question. You barely know me, so why are you going out of your way to make sure I find the perfect place to stay?"

"I have this sixth sense about people," Dani said. "I know immediately if I like them and if we'll be friends. Trust me, we will be."

Sydney understood the sixth-sense bit. Her intuition about people at first sight was frequently right on target. Right now her intuitions were making her nervous.

She had an inexplicable feeling that if she moved onto the Double K Ranch, she might be putting the three people with her at this table in danger.

But Jackson had told her to get involved. She could at least go see the accommodations.

"You've talked me into it," Sydney said. "Only I'll take my own car and follow Riley. Makes no sense for the men to have to drive me back into town."

"I'll call Esther and let her know you're on your way."

Sydney was not at all sure this was the best way to find Rachel. Perhaps working with Jackson wasn't such a good idea after all.

RILEY DROVE AT a safe speed for following. They stayed to back roads, making a couple of turns before leaving the shops and surrounding neighborhood of homes that looked as if they might date back one hundred years or more.

Sydney studied the passing scenery. Rolling hills of fenced pastureland with cattle grazing or resting beneath the shade of spreading oaks and clusters of towering pines. Ranch homes tucked behind elaborate metal gates that appeared to welcome rather than shut out visitors.

Peaceful. Pastoral. Convivial.

Had Rachel driven down this very road, alone or already in the hands of an abductor? A hunky cowboy, perhaps, who seemed exciting until he'd turned on her.

Last night she'd imagined it might be someone like Tucker, a brooding cowboy sitting alone in a noisy bar, lost in his own troubling world.

Those were not the vibes she'd picked up today. She wondered what part the change in his looks from unkempt to ruggedly virile and handsome had played in her subconscious impressions.

Lean and muscled. Dark hair. Penetrating eyes that communicated what his mouth left unsaid.

It was difficult to imagine the man was an abductor when he seemed to want nothing to do with her. Perhaps because he had a lot on his mind as he'd said. More likely she wasn't his type.

The ringing of her cell phone interrupted her thoughts. A wave of anxiety tensed her muscles. The caller's identity flashed across the car's dashboard display.

Carl Upton.

Guess he'd finally found time to call her back. "Hello, Carl."

"Glad I caught you," he said. "I just saw a news bulletin about Rachel. It asked for anyone who knows her whereabouts to contact the police at once."

"Did they show a picture?"

"Yes, but it was the one that was in the newspaper of her leaving the courthouse with the other winning attorneys last Friday. It's grainy. Hard to make out her delicate features, so I don't know how much good it's going to do."

"I'll get another one to them."

"I can't believe I'm learning about this from a news bulletin."

"You didn't. Connie Ledger called you yesterday morning."

"She said Rachel didn't show up for work that morning. I figured she just got held up in traffic."

"I left you a message to call me back. You didn't."

"I was in a meeting all day. You didn't say it was an emergency."

"Why would I even be calling you if it wasn't an emergency? What else did they say in the news bulletin."

"That it was possibly connected to some lunatic serial kidnapper."

Sydney swallowed hard. She hadn't expected the police to leak that possibility with no hard evidence to support it. "Did they say what brought them to that conclusion?"

"No, but this is starting to freak me out. You don't believe she's been kidnapped, do you?"

"I don't have any idea what's happened to her, Carl."

"C'mon, Sydney. You're FBI. You have the inside scoop. I'm just asking for a little reassurance. You don't believe she's being held captive or…" His voice trailed off.

"I don't have enough facts yet to make that call," Sydney said.

"Have you checked all the hospitals?" Carl asked. "As stressed as she was, she might have collapsed on the street somewhere."

"How would you know that Rachel was stressed? I didn't think you two were still communicating."

"We were together four years, Sydney. You

can't just turn off four years of your life like it was water from a spigot."

According to Rachel, they could and had. *I've moved on* had been her exact words.

"When was the last time you talked to Rachel?" she questioned.

"The Friday she left. I called to congratulate her on her win. That was all over the news. She got an offhand mention as being part of the defense team though not the credit I'm sure she deserved."

"I talked to her that night, as well," Sydney said. "She sounded relieved to me. Exhausted but relieved."

"Well, let me know as soon as you hear something."

"Sure. Gotta go now."

Sydney flicked on her blinker and took the same left turn Riley had. She'd go through with the visit to the Double K Ranch, but she'd be counting the minutes until she met with Jackson Clark.

If nothing else, he had an identification on the murdered woman. One piece of the puzzle was better than none.

The fear hit again, knotting in her stomach and hammering at both temples as they reached the gate for the Double K Ranch.

TRAPPED IN THE DARK, dingy dungeon, with nothing new to look at, Rachel was forced to rely on her other senses to remain sane and focused. She knew the monster's footsteps, clunking as if he were stamping around in the Western boots he'd been wearing every time he'd brought her food.

She wasn't sure if he was a real cowboy or just dressed the part. She wasn't sure of anything about him except that he was mentally unstable.

Sometimes he sat down and talked to her like they were old friends, but then out of nowhere, he'd start screaming at her, almost as if there were two men living inside his head.

The dark, dank environment made her surmise she was walled off in a back corner of a basement. The early warning that he was coming was the creaking of the stairs as he descended.

But at times she heard other footsteps and voices. She feared there were other prisoners locked up in this hellhole. She'd tried calling out once, but he'd heard her and punished her with no food until she was so hungry she could barely function.

Rachel rolled off her pallet and pulled herself to a standing position. The aches were not as unbearable as they'd been when she'd first regained consciousness but movement was still painful. The good news was that she'd improved enough that while much of her body was bruised and swollen, she was almost certain there were no broken bones or serious internal injuries.

She held on to the wall as she walked barefoot on the hard cement floor. If she didn't get some exercise her cramped muscles would atrophy.

She'd only made it halfway across the narrow space when she heard the *thump-thump-thump* of approaching footsteps on the stairs. She froze in place. He was coming.

Anxiety swelled in her chest, making it difficult to breathe. She never knew what to expect from his visits and the uncertainty was just another layer of the torture.

Sometimes, he just set her food on the floor and left without even looking at her. Other times, he stared silently at her as if she were a vile, disgusting serpent that had slithered into his space.

This time it sounded as if he were dragging something down the stairs with him. She moved to the door and pressed her right ear against it.

There were shuffling noises and then what sounded like the scrape of a door being opened.

Not her door.

"Help me. Someone, please help me."

The shrill cry was followed by what sounded like something—or someone—being hurled against a wall.

Rachel's hell had apparently gained a new guest. The monster was increasing his menagerie.

Chapter Seven

If Sydney had been telling the truth about wanting to explore the charms of the Texas Hill Country for a travel article, she would have just hit a bases-loaded home run. Riley stopped his truck in front of Esther Kavanaugh's house and she pulled in behind him.

She got out and stood for a moment, absorbing the environment. Esther Kavanaugh's sprawling white clapboard house with its dark green front door and shutters blended in with the pastoral environment. It was neither imposing nor elaborate, but had that lived-in look, warm and welcoming.

A wide porch was accented by two large wooden rockers cozied up to a round wooden table. An inviting porch swing scattered with small, colorful pillows encouraged sitting and staying awhile. Pots of blooming marigolds, vinca and geraniums added color.

A hanging hummingbird feeder was getting lots of use and butterflies fluttered among the lantana that seemed to be taking over the garden that bordered the railed porch.

Both men waited until she joined them. They walked together along the slightly cracked path to the porch.

Tucker opened the unlocked door and held it for her to enter.

"Don't you think you should knock first?" Sydney asked.

"We're family," Riley said. "Well, not biologically, but in all the ways that really matter."

Sydney would have still knocked before just walking in, not that she knew anyone who left their house wide-open.

"You should caution her to leave her door locked," Sydney said. She'd seen too much violence in her job to ever be that trusting.

"She's expecting us," Riley said. "I'm surprised she wasn't on the porch waiting to greet us as much as she loves company."

"I can see how someone could get lonesome out here with no neighbors."

"She's got plenty of neighbors," Tucker said. "They're just not in hollering distance. They're there if you need them."

"Plenty of neighbors and friends," Riley added. "And she has the full lowdown on all of them. There are no secrets in a town the size of Winding Creek."

"I'll be sure to remember that."

Tucker led the way through the house, walking too fast to allow Sydney a good look at the interior. What she saw she liked.

If the comfortable furniture, hooked rugs and collection of framed pictures were any indication of Esther's personality, Sydney could see why Dani was so fond of her.

"You've got company, Esther." Tucker's call went unanswered.

"She's probably in the garden or down at the chicken pen," Riley said. "You two can stay out of the heat. I'll go let her know we're here."

He walked out the back door, leaving them alone together again. Tucker stood at the back window that looked out over a pumpkin patch not quite ready for harvest. Not surprisingly ignoring her.

She walked over and stood beside him,

aware too quickly of his woodsy, musky scent. His virility gave him a presence that never let her forget he was all man. Strange, since she was used to a testosterone overload in her work environment.

It must be the cowboy mystique or the situation that affected her awareness of him. She had no idea what made him react so negatively toward her.

"If my staying here is going to make you uncomfortable, I'll make other plans."

He turned to face her. "Why do you think you make me uncomfortable?"

"You avoid talking to me."

"I'm not much in the mood for making small talk right now. It has nothing to do with you, so don't take it personally."

"Okay. Does that mean you don't mind my staying here?"

"Not at all. Given a choice, I can't imagine you'd want to stay anywhere else. I guarantee you'll feel the same once you get to know Esther."

"And yet you're in a huge hurry to cut out again?"

"I have business to take care of."

His phone rang. "Excuse me," he said, answering as he walked out of the room.

"Hello, Lauren."

That was all she heard before he was out of hearing distance, but the strain in his hello was a good indication that Lauren might be part of his problem. Possibly relationship trouble. That would explain a lot.

Not that she knew a lot about that. She'd never been in a serious relationship. She'd tried to convince herself she was serious about a guy a few times, but she'd only been lying to herself.

Apparently, Rachel had done the same with Carl Upton. Gone through the motions of being in love long after she'd realized she wasn't. How else would they have moved on so quickly after living together for four years?

Tucker returned just as Esther and Riley arrived back at the kitchen. Esther's smile lit up the room the second her plump body swayed into the kitchen. She set the basket of late-summer vegetables she was carrying on the counter.

"Sorry I wasn't here when you arrived. It's so hot out there I was afraid these were going to cook on the vines instead of in the pot."

"Please don't apologize," Sydney said. "It's more like I'm busting in on you and disrupting your day."

"Land sakes, honey, I've got nothing but time these days. Even the chickens are getting tired of seeing me."

"I'm sure that's not true."

Esther rubbed the palms of her hands on her jeans and extended the right one to Sydney. "I'm Esther Kavanaugh, queen of the garden and chief cook and bottle washer."

"I'm Syd Cotton. Struggling freelancer and temporarily homeless."

"That's what Dani said. You obviously made an impression on her. She was eager to make sure you have a good stay in Winding Creek."

"For sure I'll be several pounds heavier when I leave here if I spend much time in her bakery."

"Or here," Riley said. "Wait till you taste Esther's biscuits. And her peach cobbler won first place in the town's pie and cobbler making contest last month."

"Yes, but my coconut meringue pie only came in second."

"Biased judges," Tucker teased.

"My house is nothing fancy," Esther said, "but the beds are comfortable and the water's hot. Plenty of space for privacy and spreading out. I've got rooms that have been empty so long the flowers in the wallpaper are starting to droop."

"You two seem to be hitting it off," Riley said. "Syd says she's short on time, so why don't you go ahead and show her around. Pierce needs some mechanical help with his tractor again. I'll hang around with them and watch Tucker get his hands greasy."

"There is one thing," Tucker said. "Since you're a stranger around here, if you two do come to an agreement, Esther will need references."

"Of course." Syd Cotton would have the best. Lane would see to that.

Esther shook her head. "I'm not selling her the house, Tucker. If I want to have Syd as a houseguest, I guess that's my business."

Now she'd started a disagreement between Tucker and Esther. This wasn't going to work on any level.

"You're right," Tucker said. "Your house, your rules. As it should be."

That didn't mean he and his brothers wouldn't come nosing about to make sure she was acceptable. She'd have limited privacy and that would be a problem.

Once she got into the case, her maps and charts would have to be strung across the walls like huge banners so she could study them. It was the best way to see patterns.

Times and places where Rachel and the others were last seen. Places where they could have come in contact with the perp before the abductions. Any commonly shared links of interest among the women. An extensive study of their social-media habits.

At this point, studying the lifestyles of the missing women was all she'd have to go on.

"Let's start with the bedrooms," Esther suggested. "I have several to choose from, a few with their own bathrooms. And I do have wireless now. Pierce bought me one of those fancy tablets."

"Which she hates," Riley said.

"I don't hate it. Just don't need it. No sense in hanging your wash on someone else's line, and that's exactly what that social-media bologna feels like to me. Now, if you guys will excuse us, we've got business to take care of."

THE HOUSE WAS exactly what Sydney would have needed—if she actually was a freelance writer. The bedrooms were immaculate and, despite Esther's disclaimer, several of them were a bit fancy, at least when compared to the main living areas of the house. One of them even had sliding glass doors leading to a patio, a perfect place for morning coffee.

"This is my favorite of all the guest rooms," Esther said. "It wouldn't give you much room for work, but the room next to it has a writing desk. No reason you couldn't use both."

"I'm sure I could make that work."

Unfortunately, it didn't solve the privacy issue. On the other hand, the old locks on the door had keys in them, so she could keep that room locked at all times.

Even better, Esther was a delight to be around. Outspoken, glaringly honest, upbeat and witty. And a wealth of information about Winding Creek and the surrounding area.

They wound up the tour in the spacious family room. The grouping of pictures on the wall to the left of the stone fireplace captured her attention. Most appeared to be of Riley, Pierce and Tucker.

Sydney walked over for a closer look. She focused on one of the Lawrence brothers when they were much younger. The three of them on horseback, looking at home in their saddles.

"We have such great memories of those boys," Esther said. "They brought so much love into this house. I was proud of them then and even prouder now. They turned into such remarkable young men."

"Exactly how did they come to live with you?"

"Their parents died in a car crash. Tucker was only twelve, just a kid, but he tried so hard to hide all his fears and grief. I just wanted to hold him and let him know it was okay to grieve, but I gave him time to come to me. When he finally did, we cried buckets of tears."

"He was very lucky to have you," Sydney said. "All three of them were."

"I guess so. Social Services couldn't find any foster parents willing to take all three of them, so they were going to split them up. Charlie heard about that, and the next thing I knew, they were living with us. We had them for ten months before a biological uncle they'd never met before showed up."

"So, the boys had to go with him?"

"He had legal rights. We didn't. But Charlie hired a private detective to make sure they were being treated right. Their uncle was a good man."

"Charlie was your husband?"

"For fifty-three years. I loved that man every day of them. I still do. 'Spect I will till they lay me in the ground beside him."

"How long has he been dead—unless you'd rather not talk about it?"

"Oh, I've done plenty of talking about it. Talked so much people around here are tired of hearing me. They think I don't know what I'm talking about, but I do."

"What don't they believe?"

"That Charlie was murdered. In his own barn. In cold blood. They think Charlie committed suicide. But I know what I know."

A chill washed over Sydney. She didn't know Charlie or anything about him, but she knew Esther was convinced he'd been murdered.

Murdered right here on this ranch in the safe little town of Winding Creek, where even

Esther didn't bother with locking her door when she was home alone.

Where Rachel had last been seen. Evil didn't recognize havens.

"How long has he been dead?"

"A year and six months. I remember it like it was yesterday. I was on the porch, waiting on him to come to lunch. There was a big pot of beans on the stove. I'd cooked up some turnip greens from the garden and an iron skillet of corn bread to go with them. And sliced some sweet onions. All Charlie's favorites.

"I waited. He didn't come. He never came."

One huge tear made its way down Esther's right cheek, followed by an avalanche.

Sydney put an arm around her. Esther leaned against her and cried until the shoulder of Sydney's shirt was wet with her tears.

When the last of the sobs played out, Esther pulled away and dabbed at her eyes with her fists.

"I'm sorry. I didn't mean to go there but you're the only one who's given any indication you believe me about Charlie's being murdered. Seemed to tilt me back into the hurt."

"Was his death investigated?"

"Yes, but without my input. My heart

couldn't take it when I found the body. By the time I recovered from the heart attack, Sheriff Cavazos had declared the death a suicide."

"And there was no follow-up after your complaints?"

"No. Pierce and Riley both talked to the sheriff but they say there's no evidence to support murder."

Sydney knew that wasn't proof Charlie Kavanaugh hadn't been murdered. Now another young woman had been murdered and four young women were missing in this idyllic rural community.

Coincidence?

Likely, but unusual enough she couldn't ignore it.

They said their goodbyes, forgoing any decision about Syd returning as a paying houseguest.

Sydney literally ran into Tucker as she was leaving. He was coming in the front door as she was going out and they bumped against each other. It was awkward and unnerving, though she didn't know why he had such an unexplainable effect on her. It was time to move past that.

He opened the door for her and moved back. "Sorry. I seem to say that a lot with you."

"Too much," she agreed. "How about we call a truce and start over? See if we can move this into a steadier groove."

"I'm game if you are," he said. He put out his hand. "I'm Tucker Lawrence. Nice to meet you, Syd Cotton."

Her fake name. They'd be starting over with a lie between them, but with this much at stake it couldn't be helped.

She shook his hand, aware of the calluses and the strength in his grip.

"Will you be moving in tonight?" he asked.

"I haven't made any firm decisions, but I definitely won't be leaving Winding Creek for a while."

"Then perhaps you'll let me buy you dinner tonight at the Caffe Grill. Their steaks don't come anywhere near measuring up to the ones I can grill with Kavanaugh beef. However, their burgers are still delicious and their fish tacos go down mighty easy with a beer."

He was serious about starting over. She felt guilty knowing that if she met him in town it would be all business for her. Everything would be until Rachel was safe.

She couldn't think beyond that, but she would like to pick Tucker's brain and see if he and his brothers' take on Charlie's death differed from Esther's.

"I'll be working this afternoon. It might be late before I can get away."

"That's not a problem for me. I'm a night owl myself."

"I thought cowboys got up with the sun."

"Not all of us. I'll give you my phone number. Call me if you want to get together. If you don't, no problem."

"I'll call you by seven," she said. "One way or another, I'll call and let you know."

She put his number into her phone and walked away. Doubt crept into her mind. Was she being totally honest with herself about why she wanted to see Tucker tonight?

Yes, she assured herself. This was all business as long as Rachel and the others were missing and a madman possibly held all their lives in his hands.

IT WAS A quarter past one when Sydney finally got to meet with Jackson and three of the agents she'd be working with. She resented the wasted hours in between, time that she could have been chasing down clues.

But she was not the one in control.

The meeting was in a privately owned fishing cabin overlooking Winding Creek. The creek itself was slow-moving but wide and deep enough that it looked more like a river to her.

Jackson met her at the door. He shook her hand and introduced himself. "Hope you didn't have any trouble finding this place. It's kind of hidden back in here."

"No trouble, thanks to your good directions. I did get a little worried crossing that narrow wooden bridge."

"Know what you mean, but Sheriff Cavazos assured me the bridge was safe."

"Is this his cabin?"

"Belongs to a friend of his but he said we could use it as long as we need. He would have offered us space at his office but they took in water during the spring floods and the back half of the building is undergoing major repair. Could barely hear myself think with all the racket going on."

"Other than that, how did the meeting go?" Sydney asked.

"It went well. Seems like Cavazos's got a good handle on things. At this point, he has no idea if he's dealing with one perp or more. Either way, he fears it's only a matter of time until another woman goes missing."

"Good that he realizes how urgent this is."

"No one knows that better than you. I can only imagine how difficult this is on you. If you want to back out at any time, I'll understand."

"I'm willing to see how it goes," she said. She could make no promises. Sipping coffee and talking to strangers at Dani's wasn't getting the job done.

Three male agents were sitting around a long wooden table when they joined them in the roomy kitchen. They all stood for introductions.

Allan Cullen looked to be in his midforties and explained that he'd been with the Bureau ever since he'd graduated college.

They had that in common. She was twenty-seven and had been with the FBI for six years, having graduated from UT in three.

Second guy was Tim Adams, whom she'd met before but hadn't run into in several years. She knew him better by reputation. He'd helped capture a well-known serial killer in the Northwest a few years back and had been instrumental in cracking several big cases since then.

Rene Foster was the oldest of the bunch, around fifty, she'd guess. His hair was beginning to gray. His hairline was seriously receding, but he'd managed to stay in good physical condition.

That left her. "I'm Sydney Maxwell," she said, "and thrilled to be part of this team."

"You're the profiling queen," Rene said. "You pegged the description of the Swamp Strangler with almost nothing to go on and then tracked him down. Impressed the hell out of us old-timers."

"Thank you," she said.

"Sydney's going to play a slightly different role in this investigation," Jackson said. "She's going to be officially unofficial."

"That's a new one on me," Allan said. "How does that work?"

"She'll be working in the background, using all the information you feed her and giving us the benefit of her expertise but not doing any fieldwork."

"Why is that?" Rene asked.

"Her sister is one of the missing women."

All three of the men turned to stare at Sydney in total silence. Rene finally broke the quiet. "I'm really sorry to hear about your sister. Really sorry."

The others joined in with their condolences, but their expressions revealed more than their concerns about her feelings.

"If any of you have questions about her role, we should clear that up now," Jackson said.

"I would think keeping this objective would be difficult for Sydney," Rene said.

"Sydney, do you want to answer that?" Jackson said.

"I'm not sure I'm ever totally objective when dealing with perps who are abducting and killing women. I don't expect it to affect my judgment."

Not that she could guarantee that.

"If the perp finds out you are the sister to one of his victims, wouldn't that put you in more danger?" Tim asked.

"If danger was an issue, I wouldn't work for the FBI," she assured him. That she was certain of.

"I remember an interview you gave after the Swamp Strangler case," Tim added. "You explained that seemingly casual comments made by the victims' families had given you the most insight into the mind of the killer."

"I can't deny that," she said.

"If that becomes an issue, we can always move her into the field," Jackson said.

In her mind it was already an issue. But how could she turn down access to all of the information the FBI would have at its fingertips?

"Makes sense," Allan said.

Only with everything out in the open, it made even less sense to Sydney. Being officially unofficial sounded more like being close to the loop but not really in it.

"There's bottled water and soft drinks in the fridge, some chips and other snacks on the counter," Jackson told them, "and a fresh pot of coffee. Help yourself at any time. This is going to be a long afternoon."

The guys got coffee. Sydney chose a bottle of water. Her nerves were edgy enough without adding more caffeine to her system.

"Now to get down to a few of the organizational details. This cabin will serve as my living quarters and our joint office while we do the initial investigating. We will be working closely with Sheriff Cavazos and his deputies."

"What do they have for us so far?" Rene asked.

"Computer printouts of all the missing persons reports and information on the recently identified body. Tim is going to fill you in on the latest information not included in the printouts."

Jackson sat down and Tim stood and took the lead. "The body has been identified as Sara Goodwin, a sixteen-year-old runaway last known to be living on the streets of San Antonio. Examination of her body indicated severe trauma with bruises and lacerations around the head and face. Evidence suggested she'd been killed somewhere else and her body taken to the wooded area where she'd been found. Naked. Her head shaved."

The other missing women were between the ages of twenty-two and thirty-two, Rachel being the oldest. They were all from different towns, were not believed to know one another and were all believed to have been abducted within sixty miles of the fishing cabin they occupied right now.

Sydney scribbled a few notes as she listened

though she knew they would also get this information in printed form. This meeting was meant to trigger the brainstorming process. Evidence would continue to be gathered and discussed from every angle.

Sydney understood the process but hearing Rachel talked about in the abstract was making her dizzy and nauseous. Not that the others were heartless. Far from it. They just weren't talking about their own flesh and blood.

They spent the next few hours going over the next steps in the investigation process, deciding on priorities, tossing ideas back and forth like rubber balls.

She had no quarrel with Jackson's decisions and leadership, but she was beginning to feel less and less like a full member of the team.

She was on the outside because she was too closely involved. But that was exactly why she couldn't sit back for even a second. She couldn't simply digest and analyze what they shot to her.

Profiling was 10 percent knowledge and practice and 90 percent intuition, at least it was the way she went at it. First impressions, instant reactions to how and what family members and friends reported about the victims, getting a feel that something was off-kilter.

She had to be neck deep in the investigation to trust those.

It was quarter to seven before she had a chance to talk privately with Jackson.

He poured himself another cup of coffee and brought it to the small kitchen table where she was sitting. "I think we're off to a good start," he said. "I know you'll need additional information but that's coming."

"We need it like yesterday," she said.

"Always. Did you pick up anything of interest we should be looking into?"

She explained her meeting with Dani Lawrence and her visit to Esther Kavanaugh's house.

"Interesting," he commented. "Esther's name came up in my conversation with Sheriff Cavazos this morning. He said she's a good source of information for most everything that goes on in the town and larger community."

"Did he mention that her husband died less than two years ago?"

"No, that didn't come up."

"Esther's convinced he was murdered though the death was ruled a suicide."

"Family members frequently have difficulty accepting a loved one took their own life."

She knew Jackson was right about that, yet Esther had seemed so sure and didn't seem the type who'd spare herself from the truth no matter how painful.

"Esther has offered to rent me a room, or rather, she's offered to rent Syd Cotton a room."

"Are the facilities adequate?"

"More than adequate."

"Then by all means you should take her up on that. Spend time with her. Learn all you can. The Bureau will pick up the tab. Who else lives in the house?"

"No one, although she has a guest now, a man she was foster mother to some years back." Sydney explained the connection to the Lawrence brothers.

"Sounds like you'll be in good hands at the Double K Ranch."

Being in good hands was the last thing she needed now. She had no choice but to level with Jackson Clark.

"I really appreciate the opportunity to work with you and the other members of the team and with the local authorities, but I have to turn you down."

His eyebrows arched. "You asked to be included."

"I thought it was what I wanted, but I understand now why it's a bad idea to have someone personally involved working on a case."

"Care to explain?"

"I have to do this my way, not with my hands tied by the FBI or by local law enforcement."

"Whether you're official or on your own, you can't just go out and ignore the laws," Jackson said. "Do that and you'll never work for the Bureau again."

"If that's what it takes to save my sister's life, so be it. But I do still have all the rights of a private citizen."

"You have more than that," Jackson said. "And you drive a damn hard bargain. I want you on the team. We *need* you on the team. And you need access to our resources."

"I don't want to feel like I'm an outsider looking in," she said. "Rachel's my sister. I need some autonomy."

"You've got it. Now just pretend I'm the boss and let's find this perp and put him away."

"You are the boss," she said. "And thanks."

"If you've got a few more minutes, I'd like to hear even more about your sister, Rachel, and her job as a defense attorney. I don't want to assume she's the victim of a serial abductor and overlook a murderous felon she's come across in her work."

"A very good point," she agreed. Jackson took extensive notes as they talked.

By the time Sydney checked her watch it was a half hour past seven. She'd missed her deadline for making the call to Tucker. Probably for the best. Just the fact that she wanted to see him proved it was a bad idea.

Chapter Eight

Tucker dropped in Caffe's Bar and Grill a few minutes after six. He took a seat at the bar and ordered a draft beer. He wasn't expecting a call this early from Syd. Actually, he didn't really expect her to call at all.

Worse, he wasn't sure why he cared. Not that she wasn't gorgeous and fascinating, but he didn't know where his life was going in the immediate future. It would be the worst time ever to get involved in a new relationship.

He shifted on his stool to get a better look at the TV off to the left of the bar. The sound was muted but the captions below the picture made it clear they were talking about the body of the murdered girl found practically in the neighborhood.

Then the screen skipped to a shot of Rachel

Maxwell, the San Antonio attorney last seen in Winding Creek a little over a week ago.

The peaceful, small town was grabbing headlines again. Which likely explained why the place was full on a Tuesday night. He scanned the room and figured about half of the customers were reporters.

The waitress set his beer in front of him. He took a sip and his mind went back to his own dilemma. Either show up for the competition in Tulsa next Friday or lose his momentum and reduce his chances to make it to the championship rounds in Vegas come December.

Images of Rod's head being repeatedly stamped into the hard dirt floor of the arena darted through his mind. On an incredible high one moment, the cheering crowd, the heightening danger, the thrill of winning against terrific odds.

Seconds later, it was all gone forever.

Tucker struggled to shove the thoughts out of his mind as he finished his beer. By seven o'clock the restaurant section was starting to clear out. The locals ate early.

The bar was more crowded than ever.

He checked his phone to be certain he hadn't missed Sydney's call. He hadn't. He dropped money for his drink and a generous tip on the bar and surrendered his bar stool to the next thirsty customer.

He wasn't even sure why he'd come back to Winding Creek now. He hadn't mentioned Rod's death to his brothers, and apparently, no one else had, either.

Winding Creek had its own hurricane of news hitting right now.

He ended up at Hank's, where he took the same table he'd sat at last night. The bar was jumping tonight. He glanced over to the table where Syd had been sitting last night. Three guys in dark-colored slacks and white shirts unbuttoned at the neck were sipping martinis. Almost certainly not locals.

The same waitress he'd had last night stopped by for his order. "Let's see. Jack Daniel's, wasn't it. Over ice."

"Good memory," he said. "Two shots."

"Do you remember that woman who was in here last night. Sandy-haired blonde. Sitting by herself. Really attractive. She came over and talked to you before she left."

"I remember. What about her?"

"I think she's an undercover cop. She

showed me a picture of a woman and asked if I'd seen her in here."

"Had you?" Tucker asked.

"No, but I know who the woman in the picture was now. She's Rachel Maxwell, the attorney from San Antonio who they keep talking about and showing her picture on the news."

"You could be right."

"What's really scary is that if Rachel Maxwell was in here right before she disappeared, the man who kidnapped her might have been in here, too," the waitress said. "He might have abducted her from the parking lot. I mean, if that's the case, it could have just as easily been me."

He couldn't argue that. "You should have the bouncer walk you to your car tonight."

She nodded. "I'm going to do just that. Still, it's super scary."

If Betts was right, it also meant that Syd had been lying to all of them today.

His cell phone vibrated. He pulled it from his pocket and checked the caller ID.

Number Unavailable.

He took it anyway.

"Hello."

"Hi, it's Syd Cotton. I know it's late but I wanted to let you know that I didn't forget. I had to work later than expected. Is it too late to take you up on your dinner invitation?"

"Not at all." He wouldn't miss this conversation for the world.

SYDNEY FRESHENED UP as well as she could in the bathroom at the fishing cabin before driving straight to Caffe's. The area was so crowded tonight she had to park near Dani's bakery and walk around the corner to the restaurant.

As soon as she entered, she spotted Tucker seated alone at a table near the center of the large, open serving area. He waved.

Anxiety balled in her stomach. She had to face him with the truth after feeding him her fake persona. He hadn't trusted her originally; now she'd prove his suspicions true. He'd be angry, and inexplicably that bothered her far more than it should.

If he gave her the opportunity, she'd level with him. And then they'd go their separate ways likely to never see each other again.

Tucker stood and held her chair while she

sat down. With Texas men, especially cowboys, manners never went out of vogue.

The waitress appeared almost immediately to take her drink order. She ordered a glass of Chardonnay. Tucker was already half through an icy mug of beer.

He picked up his menu. “Are you hungry?”

“Not particularly,” she admitted. The only thing she’d eaten since the breakfast croissant at Dani’s Delights was a small pack of chips she’d washed down with a diet soda hours earlier.

That didn’t mean her stomach was up to digesting food.

“Can we talk before we order?” she asked.

“Sure.” He stared at her, his eyes burning into hers with an intensity that made her hands grow clammy. “Why don’t we start with your explaining why you lied about why you’re in Winding Creek?”

He knew. She took a deep breath and exhaled slowly. “I’m sorry for the lies. They seemed necessary at the time.”

“Right. What’s a few lies to a reporter looking for a story?”

Now she was starting to get angry. The anger collided with all the fears, doubts and dread churning inside her. Her nerves were raw. She was losing control of the emotions she'd fought so hard to keep in check.

"I'm an FBI agent, Tucker. I was doing my job. I'll explain if you let me, or I can just go. Whichever works best for you."

"I'd love to hear what you have to say."

His tone had softened as well as his hardened expression. He must sense how frail her control was at this point. She struggled for the most concise way to respond. "I was officially working undercover for the Bureau, investigating the recent murder and the disappearance of women from this area."

"If you're undercover, why are you telling me this now? Why meet me here at all unless... Are you targeting someone in my family?"

"No. This isn't about your family, Tucker. It's about mine." Her voice shook on the admission.

He reached across the table and laid his much-larger hands on top of hers. The kindness was harder to handle than his coldness had been. Never had she felt so vulnerable.

Jumbled words began to tumble from her mouth. "My sister is missing. No one has seen her. They can't find her car. She's held prisoner. Or maybe she's dead."

She'd said it and now she felt as if someone was slashing her heart to shreds.

"Let's get out of here," Tucker said, assuming control as she was losing it.

She nodded, struggling to hold back the tears that were pressing hard against her eyelids. He left some bills on the table and took her arm, maneuvering her through the maze of tables and out the front door.

The tears began to fall as he led her to his truck and opened the passenger door for her. He hurried to the other side, slid under the wheel and snaked his arm around her.

Her head fell against his shoulders as any chance of calmness vanished. Sobs racked her body. She didn't try to fight them now. If she had, the heartbreaking emotions would have exploded inside her chest.

He was still holding her when the tears finally ran out. She pulled away, suddenly embarrassed at her show of weakness.

"Thanks for holding me somewhat together," she murmured. "I don't recall ever being such a train wreck."

"You had that one coming. My attitude certainly didn't help, either."

He started the truck engine.

"Where are we going? My car is just around the corner. I can walk to it."

"Your car is fine where it is for now. We're going to your motel to pick up your things, and then I'm taking you to the Double K Ranch. You need to unwind with some comfort food and a good, strong drink."

"I can get that back inside the Caffe's Grill."

"Too noisy. You also need a comfortable bed in a quiet environment. Have you had an hour of sound sleep since you learned about your sister?"

"Sure. Maybe two hours. But I'm not sure I'm up to going through why I'm really in town with Esther tonight."

"You won't have to. I'll take care of that."

"What makes you think she'd want me there once she finds out I'm on a mission to track a dangerous criminal?"

"You're on a mission to save your sister and others. Esther has the biggest heart in the world. She'll not only empathize, she'll do anything she can to help you." He reached for her hand and squeezed it. “So will I, Sydney. All you have to do is let me.”

“You’re leaving tomorrow,” she reminded him.

“I’ve had a change of plans.”

“Because you think I can’t handle this alone?”

“No. You have twice the courage I do. Maybe I’ll learn something from you.”

She didn’t believe that for a moment and it wouldn’t change a thing if she did. She had to go this alone. But the meltdown had been real. She had to have at least a few hours’ sleep if she was to remain sharp and focused.

Too tired to argue and not sure she wanted to, she was relieved the decision had been made for her. She’d be spending tonight on the Double K Ranch.

SYDNEY EXPLAINED THE full situation to Tucker as he drove her to the ranch. How and when she’d found out her sister was missing. How the last place Rachel had left a paper trail was in Dani’s Delights. Why she’d tried to make conversation with him that first night at Hank’s.

Tucker was a good listener, quick on the

uptake. A nice guy from a great family. More reason why she couldn't drag Esther or any of the Lawrences into this investigation.

Whenever a killer was involved, so was danger that reached out in all directions.

By the time they were approaching the gate to the Double K Ranch, Tucker was concluding a call to Esther to let her know that Syd was with him and would be staying in one of the guest rooms tonight.

He apologized for waking her and encouraged her not to get up. They could talk in the morning.

Sydney couldn't hear the other end of the conversation, but from Tucker's responses, she'd guess that Esther was pleased.

Tucker concluded the call and stopped at the gate.

"That was easy enough," he said. "Esther has already put out clean towels and soaps and turned down the sheets in her patio suite, as she calls it."

"She still thinks I'm doing a travel article. She deserves to know the real reason I'm staying under her roof."

"No point in getting into all of that tonight.

She said she'd leave it to me to show you to your room, unless we need her."

"I suppose that is better than confronting her with the details about Rachel tonight. I'm glad she doesn't feel she has to get up and welcome me."

"I suspect there's a bit of deviousness in her decision to leave us on our own."

"Esther, devious? In what way?"

"You'll figure it out. Now, how about jumping out and unlatching the gate for me? Passenger's chore. Part of the cowboy code."

"Yes, sir."

Sydney hopped out of the truck, unlatched the gate and swung it open, stepping carefully across the cattle gap. A slight breeze ruffled her hair, tossing a few strands onto her face. The air smelled of fresh-mowed hay and the honeysuckle that grew in trailing clumps across the barbwire fence.

She breathed deeply, sucking in the fragrances and the sounds that surrounded her. Katydids, the howl of coyotes off in the distance, a horse neighing.

A sudden wave of confidence swept through her. She was a trained FBI agent and woman on a mission. There was no time for wallowing in fear or dread. All her energy had to be spent on finding Rachel.

Evidently the hard bout of sobs in Tucker's arms had functioned like a release valve, relieving the pressure before she exploded and became useless in the investigation.

Suddenly she was starving.

Tucker drove through the gate and she closed and latched it again before climbing back into the truck with new fervor.

He gunned the engine and they kicked up a cloud of dust as they raced down the dirt road to the house.

Hold on, Rachel. With a little help from Tucker Lawrence, I'm coming as fast as I can.

TUCKER TENDED THE thick slices of bacon, turning them, while Sydney sliced a juicy, ruby-red tomato, no doubt fresh from Esther's summer garden.

He checked the fridge for condiments. "Do you want anything on yours besides the BLT and mayo?"

"Just bread," she said.

"White or wheat?"

"Wheat, if Esther has it."

He checked the bread canister. "You're in luck."

Bringing her here had been the right thing to do. There had been no more tears. The speed with which she'd pulled herself together after her crying frenzy was amazing.

She was a strong woman. It would take that to be in her line of work. But now it was her sister in danger and the strain of that could take down the strongest. He'd seen what emotional strain could do to a man many times on the circuit. A divorce. A family illness. Seeing a rider sustain a serious injury.

Any distraction could rob a man of the competitive edge. A bull rider could hit bottom in a matter of weeks.

His thoughts took a downturn and once again he was back in the hospital, staring into Rod's cold, blank stare as the last of life escaped his jerking body.

Rod, like Tucker, had known his choice of career involved risk, but then, so did many other professions. Just being alive involved risk.

Sydney scooted between him and the range and speared a slice of bacon from the grease and onto a paper-towel-lined plate.

"Falling down on my job," Tucker said. "Sorry about that."

"You looked deep in thought. You're not having regrets, are you?" she asked. "You can always drive me back to the motel, just not before I devour my sandwich."

"I have a world of regrets," Tucker said, "but not about you being here."

"In that case, you keep the bacon from burning and I'll toast the bread."

"You've got a deal." He also opened a couple of beers and set them on the table. "There may be wine if you'd rather have it," he said. "I only like grapes in jelly, so I'm not sure what Esther keeps in the vino department."

"I'm not much of a drinker, but a cold beer sounds good right now."

She was halfway through her sandwich and he was on his last bite before either of them started a new conversation.

"This may be the best sandwich I've ever had," she said.

"More likely, you were famished."

"That, too. This is the first time I've had any kind of appetite since I got the call that my sister was missing."

"And I've done nothing but eat since getting

to the Double K. Cooking is one of Esther's great joys. Fortunately, she's terrific at it."

"I can tell she thinks of you and your brothers as family."

"We all three feel the same about her. She and Charlie didn't just give us a place to live when our parents died. They gave us a home."

"I felt the love in this house the first time I walked through the door."

"My brothers and I were drowning in grief when we arrived for the first time, but I'm guessing we felt the love, too. I have countless great memories from the ten months we were here."

"And now your brothers have come back here to settle down and raise a family. Do you ever think of moving here permanently?"

"I haven't really considered moving anyplace permanently."

"So you just ramble from town to town and ranch to ranch?"

He knew she was only making small talk as an escape from the horrors of her life. No reason to lie about his profession but he wasn't going to pile his problems on top of hers.

"I drive from rodeo to rodeo for most of the year," he said. "I'm on the PBR circuit."

"I have no idea what that means."

"I'm a professional bull rider."

She choked on a sip of beer. "You ride bulls for a living?"

"For a living. Such as it is."

There were years he'd struggled to come up with the entry fees. However, he had no complaints about his earnings this year.

"I've come across bull riding a few times while channel surfing," Sydney admitted. "It looks incredibly dangerous."

"Does that mean you have never been to a rodeo?"

"Afraid so."

"We'll have to change that."

She managed a smile. "Maybe we will."

He'd love to take her to a rodeo, though it might not be him atop the bull.

"Is Charlie Kavanaugh the one who got you interested in bull riding?"

"Charlie introduced my brothers and me to everything there is to know about the cowboy life. How to avoid getting kicked by your horse and to always drink upstream from the herd," he joked.

"And how to ride a bull, at age twelve?"

"The bulls were tamer than the kind of

monsters I meet on the circuit, but you gotta start young if you want to be good at it."

"What else did Charlie teach you?"

"How to shoot and handle a gun. Branding. Proper care of our horse. The list goes on and on. Basically, he made damn sure we learned about honor and the cowboy code."

"What's the cowboy code?"

"Basic rules to live by."

"Such as?"

"Never leave spur marks on a horse's flesh. Women should be respected and protected. Put away your horse before you put away your dinner. There were lots of them, but the one at the top of the list was a cowboy always keeps his word."

"Charlie sounds like a man among men."

"Yep. He and Esther. Good folks. That's what they call people like that around here. Charlie was one of the best. He had friends among the richest ranchers in these parts and the poorest. Treated them all the same."

"Who is the richest rancher in this area?"

Her tone grew serious and he knew her focus had moved back to Rachel. Her mind had likely never left there.

"Dudley Miles has the most land and the

most cattle. I can't vouch for his bank account, but I hear he burns dollar bills instead of wood in their five fireplaces."

She smiled and took another sip of her beer. "Not only a bull rider, but a BSer, I see."

"Burning bills is a slight exaggeration. The house with five fireplaces is fact."

"Is that the same Dudley Miles who went to prison for the death of his grandson?"

"Yeah. Were you in on that investigation?"

"No. The local police handled that, but it was on cable news 24/7 at the time. Refresh my memory. Exactly how did that go down?"

"Dudley and Millie's bratty, irresponsible daughter, Angela, had a baby. It never came out who the baby's father was, but from all accounts Dudley and Millie were raising the kid. Angela was not big on dependability."

"Spoiled?"

"Totally, and had a drug problem. One weekend Angela was home alone with the two-year-old. She overdosed on cocaine and passed out. When she came to, she found the toddler on the kitchen floor, not breathing."

"Now I remember," Sydney said. "Angela Miles got scared and dumped the kid's body in a wooded area. She told her parents and everyone else he'd been kidnapped."

"Right," Tucker said. "Then when the body was found and the kidnapping lie lost all credibility, Dudley took the blame to protect his daughter, claimed he was totally responsible."

"But now the grandfather is out of prison and Angela is serving time for neglect leading to death and lying to the authorities to cover it up."

"About time. It's a long, tragic story for another night, but there's a reason why I know so much about that event. A few months back, Dani and Riley played an unintended role in Angela's finally going to prison. In the process, Dani was almost killed. Get her to tell you that story someday."

"I will." Sydney stared at the half-empty beer bottle she was rocking back and forth. The remaining fourth of her sandwich apparently forgotten.

"Where was the boy's body found?" she asked.

"A few miles from Dudley's spread, probably not far from where the news reporter said Sara Goodwin's body was found."

"Who owns that land?"

"An investor out of Los Angeles owns the land where Dudley's grandson was found. He's not from around here, and if I've ever heard his name, I don't remember it. I only know that much because Dudley has been trying to buy it from him for years. It borders the west side of Dudley's spread."

"Do you think he also owns the land where Sara Goodwin's body was found?"

"I'm not sure if his land extends that far west or not."

Syndey stood and carried their plates to the kitchen. "I want to see the area where both their bodies were found. Do you think you can locate those spots?"

"I can take you right to the area where Dudley's grandson's body was found. I only have a general idea of the other crime scene, but we can probably find it. I'm sure it's roped off with police tape."

Tucker wiped down the range and counter while Sydney rinsed the dishes and slid them into the dishwasher. "I'd like to be there by daybreak," she said, "before either area is barraged with reporters."

"That's manageable."

"I don't expect you to get involved, Tucker.

You can drive me into town to pick up my car, and then I'll follow you to the locations. You can stay in your truck while I look around."

"What do you expect to find?"

"Whatever's there to be found."

He suspected that would be deer, rabbits and possibly a rattlesnake or two. But intensity burned in Sydney's eyes again, the urgency to find her sister riding her nerves.

"You need to get some sleep," he said. "Dawn comes early. Come on. I'll walk you back to your bedroom."

She didn't put up an argument.

She stopped at the door to the guest room and turned to look up at him. Her bluish-green eyes glowed from the emotional fire that blazed inside her. Her full sensuous mouth opened in a slight smile.

"Thanks for helping me make it through the meltdown," she whispered.

"My pleasure."

She trailed the fingers of her right hand down his arm. Her touch released a stampede of desires, all hitting him right between the thighs.

He'd never wanted to take a woman in his arms more.

He held back, knowing the timing was probably all wrong for her.

"See you at sunrise," she whispered. And then she opened her door and disappeared behind it.

"IT SHOULD BE light enough to see by the time we get to the first spot," Tucker said. "If not, I have a superbright flashlight in my truck bed with all my other gear."

"Which one do we hit first?" she asked.

"The spot where Dudley's grandson's body was discovered, if that works for you. We'll come to it first."

"Okay." She sipped from the travel cup filled with strong black coffee Tucker had handed her on their way to the truck.

"It may be a waste of time," she admitted. "There's no reason to think there's any connection between where Angela Miles dumped a body and the current crimes."

"For what it's worth, I concur with you on that."

"Still, it's hard to ignore the strange coincidence of two bodies from unrelated crimes turning up in such close proximity, especially on the outskirts of such a quiet, safe town like Winding Creek."

Trust your instincts. Always pay attention to anything that just doesn't feel right.

She'd learned that early in her FBI career and found it to be true more often than not.

"I know you've considered all the odds and know far more about this than I do," Tucker said. "But isn't there a strong chance that Rachel's disappearance isn't connected to any of this? A chance that she might not have been abducted at all? I mean, you read books where people have a minor stroke or fall and hit their head and get amnesia."

"Anything is possible." Her heart and her brain were convinced otherwise. Besides, the FBI would continue to explore those options for all four of the missing women.

It was the chance that Rachel and the others were in immediate and deadly danger that drove Sydney. That wouldn't abate until the missing were found.

They drove the next few miles in silence. Tucker was still basically a stranger, but she was glad he hadn't let her talk him out of coming with her.

The blacktop road took a sharp curve and

then began a steady incline. Tucker slowed and turned right onto a rutted dirt road that quickly disappeared into a heavily wooded area. The canopy of leaves and lush pine needles shut out the dawn's light, turning everything the dark purplish color of an ugly bruise.

The road began to disintegrate, becoming more rock than dirt. Eventually, it vanished completely in front of a crumbling chimney where a house had once been.

"This is the end of the line," Tucker said as he killed the engine. "The body was found somewhere between here and the waterfall."

Sydney didn't see a waterfall, but as she climbed out of the truck she heard the splash and gurgle of moving water.

Tucker retrieved the flashlight and a machete from the back of the truck. He handed her the flashlight. "I'll walk ahead of you and try to clear you a path through the worst of the undergrowth."

"Is it this dense all the way to the waterfall?"

"No, but don't expect too much from the waterfall. It may not be much more than a trickle at the end of a scorching summer."

"I didn't realize you were that familiar with the area."

"I'm not, but it's starting to come back to me now that we're here. Charlie brought us deer hunting in here a couple of times. Pierce got his first buck here."

"Shooting and riding bulls as a boy of twelve. I'm starting to see how you chose such a dangerous way to make a living."

She aimed the flashlight's beam at the ground in front of her as she maneuvered over and between clumps of prickly brush, snake-like vines and fallen limbs. Without Tucker wielding the machete, the old path would be almost impossible to navigate.

She felt something crawling on her arm. She shivered and looked down at the biggest spider she'd ever seen. Her heart seemed to stop as she knocked the dark, hairy monster off her arm and into the thick brush at her feet.

She hadn't expected anything this creepy. The howling of coyotes and the husky croaks of bullfrogs provided the soundtrack for what felt like a scene from a B-rated horror movie.

Yet a young mother had chosen this spot to dump the body of her toddler son, and then let her own father go to jail for her callous crime.

When Rachel was safe again, Sydney would make a trip to the prison to visit Angela Miles. She'd be an interesting and no doubt informative case study for profiling.

The trees thinned out and the sky lightened to a pale gray. Sydney turned off the flashlight and picked up her pace.

"Watch for loose rocks," Tucker cautioned. "There's a sharp drop-off just before you reach the waterfall."

"I will."

She reached the falls before him. She looked back to see what was keeping him.

He held up the machete. A headless rattlesnake dangled from the blade. "Watch out for these, too," he said. "Fortunately, my machete found it before it found me."

She heeded his advice, holding tight to the slim trunk of a leaning mulberry tree as she stretched over for a better look at the tumbling stream of water and the rocky area just beyond it where the body had been found.

Two deer stepped out of the trees and into the pool beneath the waterfall for a cool drink. And just past them at the edge of the woods was what looked like a scrap of red cloth, possibly an item of clothing.

"Tucker, come take a look at this."

"Be right there."

She let go of the tree trunk and took a step toward the edge. The ground shifted, tipping her off balance. She grabbed for a limb that was just above her head.

Her hand scraped the spiny wood as the branch splintered and split. She fell on her backside and went sliding across the surface of the hard, angled rocks, finally landing in the mud at the edge of the falling water.

Blood dripped from her skinned elbows and her back felt like she'd been sleeping on hot coals.

But from this vantage point she saw far more than the red scrap.

Her blood ran icy cold.

Chapter Nine

Tucker half crawled, half tumbled down the rocky ravine in his haste to get to Sydney. He'd seen the large, angular stone shift. In a split second he'd dropped the machete and reached for Sydney, but it had been too late.

His hand missed her arm and the soft fabric of her blouse slipped right through his fingers.

By the time he reached her, blood dripped from her elbows and her left hand.

He stooped down beside her and turned her hand palm up so he could judge the depth of the scratches. "We have to get you to a doctor."

"I don't need a doctor. Help me up," she ordered.

"You may have broken a bone or two."

"I don't think so. My rear hurts more than

anything else. Just give me a hand or move so I can get up by myself."

He ignored her demands and instead ripped off his shirt. He grabbed a bottle of water from his backpack and poured about half of it over his shirt.

"Let me have that hand again. I can at least try to clean the worst of the wounds. You've got blood running down your arm from cuts on your elbows, too." She finally cooperated and he slowly poured the remaining water over her hand and arms.

Blood still oozed from a couple of jagged scratches on her hand. He fashioned a make-shift bandage with his shirt and wrapped it around her hand, leaving the thumb free.

"Thanks," she murmured.

"This doesn't eliminate seeing a doctor."

"All it needs is some antibiotic ointment. We're staying on a ranch. Esther is bound to have a first-aid kit around there somewhere."

"You may need a tetanus shot."

"I had a booster two months ago. The FBI sees to things like that." She scooted away from him and tried to get up without putting pressure on her hand.

He took her right hand and helped her to a

standing position. "What was it you wanted me to see before you fell?"

She brushed off the seat of her jeans and pointed to a scrap of red that seemed to be caught in the low branches of a persimmon tree.

"Stay here, and I'll go check it out," he said.

Unsurprisingly, she didn't stay but followed him as he splashed through the shallow water to the other side of the ravine.

She pulled the material from the tree and held it up in front of her. "It's a women's blouse. It hasn't been here long enough to turn black from the elements."

"It's summer," he reminded her. "It could have been left here by teenagers having a little summer fun beneath the falls."

"It could be," she said. She folded it and handed it to him. "Put it in your backpack for now in case the blood seeps through my fancy bandage."

"Are you ready to tackle the trek back to the truck?"

"Not yet."

She scanned the area around the falls and then started walking away from the side where she'd fallen. The gorge was not as steep on that side but the trees were and the underbrush was thicker. Worse, his machete was at the top of the other side of the ravine.

She swatted at a mosquito around her face.

"As soon as we leave this clearing the mosquitoes will get much worse," he cautioned.

"Mosquitoes, spiders, snakes. I can't believe anyone would come here for afternoon delight."

She stamped a few feet farther. He hurried to catch up with her before she disappeared into the thick foliage.

"Oh, no!"

He raced to her side. "What is it?"

She pointed to a spot a few feet in front of her. "What does that look like to you?"

"The first rays of morning sun glinting off fancy taillights." He swallowed the curse that flew to mind. "How in the hell did someone get a vehicle down here?"

"And why?" Sydney added.

It was easy to tell it was dread and not curiosity that edged her voice.

The incline grew steeper and he took her arm to steady her as they approached the wreckage. The body of the car was almost invisible until they were close enough to touch it, hidden by the branches and the trunks of young trees it had knocked down as it plummeted.

He lifted a large limb off the roof. “A late-model SUV,” he noted.

She trembled. “That’s Rachel’s car.”

“Are you sure?”

She didn’t answer but pushed past him and tried to open the dented driver’s-side door. When it wouldn’t budge, she peered through the dirty windows.

“I must have dropped the flashlight when I fell. I need it. I can’t see inside.”

“Let me try the door,” he said.

She moved away. He tried the back door and it opened easily.

“Careful what you touch,” she cautioned. “There could be fingerprints inside where it’s dry and not exposed to the elements.”

As apprehensive as she was, she was on top of her game. Tucker took a quick look inside. No body. No obvious bloodstains. He breathed easier and stepped back while she crawled inside the back seat. When she got out, she leaned against the car with her good hand and took a few deep breaths before speaking.

“Do you have your phone with you?”

He reached in his pocket and handed it to her.

Seconds later, she had Jackson Clark on the phone and she was back in control. Nothing wimpy about FBI agent Sydney Maxwell.

"AS SOON AS I get cleaned up and properly bandaged, I want to pay a visit to Dudley Miles," Sydney announced.

"Fine by me. I like the man, but I don't see what you're going to get out of it."

"Hopefully the same kind of confidence in him you have. I'm not accusing him of anything, but the strange coincidences are becoming a frightening pattern. How do you explain Rachel's wrecked car being found in almost the same spot as his grandson's body was found?"

"Dudley had nothing to do with his grandson's death or the disposal of his body. The woman who did is in prison."

True, if all the suppositions in that case were true. But what if they weren't? What if someone else was involved? What if the guilty person had never been arrested or even accused?

She and Tucker had spent an hour at the

waterfall discussing the case with Jackson, Agent Rene and Sheriff Cavazos. Jackson had called Cavazos in an effort to keep local law enforcement involved. Cavazos was as insistent as Tucker that Dudley Miles was spotlessly clean.

Her conscience wouldn't let it go.

"It's also urgent I talk to Dani," Sydney said. "She may have been the last person to see Rachel before she disappeared."

"What about stopping at an emergency care clinic? There's one on the highway just past where they put in the new dollar store."

"I'm not running to a clinic for a few scratches. Like I said, I'm sure Esther has first-aid supplies. You'd have to living on a ranch, wouldn't you?"

"Yep. And if that doesn't do the trick, I can call a vet. They make house calls."

"Ha. Ha."

She shifted in the seat and put her hand to the small of her back.

"You must be sore after that fall," Tucker said.

"Nothing an aspirin or two can't fix."

And a week in a back brace. But she'd

worked hurt plenty of times when there was not nearly as much at stake.

Her next hurdle would be explaining everything to Esther. Not only was Sydney not a sweet and harmless travel writer, she might bleed all over her sheets.

All small stuff. The only thing that really mattered was finding Rachel and the rest of the missing. Her hand was already on the door handle when Tucker stopped at the gate to the Double K Ranch.

"I've got it," Tucker said. "A real cowboy never lets the bloody wounded do the work."

"More of the cowboy code?"

"If it's not, it should be."

She watched him unlatch the gate and swing it open. It was midmorning now and the sun glistened on his shirtless shoulders and chest. His muscles rippled. Bull-rider muscles, and he'd be back to that soon.

But for now, he was making it clear he was all hers. The shocker was that she was thankful to have him around.

TUCKER PLOPPED DOWN on the top slat of the corral and hooked the heels of his boots on the bottom slat. He'd left Sydney back at the house getting her wounds cared for by Esther and Pierce's wife, Grace. No doubt, she was going through the same grilling he'd just endured with his brothers.

"Now you know as much as I do about the investigation," Tucker said.

Pierce pushed his straw work hat to the back of his head. "Sydney sounds like one smart, tough woman, but this has got to be really rough on her. Glad she finally confided in you."

"Amazing that she and Dani connected so fast," Riley said, "or was that more than coincidental?"

"The scant paper trail Sydney has on Rachel indicates that that the bakery is the last place she used her credit card."

"Does Dani know that?" Riley asked.

"Not yet. She will soon. We're heading that way soon. Sydney is hoping Dani remembers her and might know if she was alone or with someone. Any clue would be helpful."

"Film from the security camera might show that, even if Dani doesn't remember," Riley said.

"This is really starting to hit close to home," Pierce said. "I'm not sure I want Grace running the roads by herself or just with Jaci until the freaky lunatic is caught."

"And I may hang around the bakery a little later in the morning," Riley said. "Keep my eye on things until the customers start piling in and Constance leaves for school."

Tucker jumped off the fence, his boots digging into the carpet of grass as he landed. "It's guaranteed I won't be telling Sydney what she can and can't do."

"She's FBI," Riley said. "What do you expect?"

"Exactly what is going on between you two?" Pierce asked.

"Basically, what I've already told you. I forced my way into her life and she hasn't kicked me out yet."

"It's a little more than that," Pierce said. "You arrived here in a serious funk."

"Was it that obvious?"

Riley socked him in the arm. "Was it ever, bro? You weren't yourself at all. We figured it had to be woman problems to bring you that low."

He'd come here for his brothers' feedback on the indecision that plagued him. Now was probably as good a time as any to talk about it.

"You remember me talking about my rodeo buddy Rod the last time I was here?"

"Yeah," Pierce said. "You said he was one of the best bull riders on the circuit this year and a really great guy. Said he was giving you your roughest competition this year."

"He was. He died last week."

Riley dropped his favorite curse word when not in mixed company. "Was it work related?"

"Yeah. Six seconds into the ride on the meanest and biggest bull in the night's contest. His form was perfect. The crowd was on its feet. This might have been the closest any of them had ever come to seeing a perfect score."

"Man, that had to be tough to watch."

"The worst."

"At least he died doing something he loved," Riley said.

"He died leaving a wife with no husband and three young children with no father. After watching Rod take his last breath, I had to drive to their house in Lubbock and give them the tragic news."

"That explains and justifies the funk you were in," Pierce said. "Wouldn't be much of a man if that didn't get to you."

"Then I must be a hell of a man."

Riley put his arm around Tucker's shoulders. "I've never doubted that."

"Watching Rod die has made me rethink a lot of my life choices."

"Does that mean you're thinking of giving up bull riding?" Pierce asked.

"I'm considering it. I haven't made a decision."

"That's a big one," Riley said. "I was worried if I could give up my rambling ways when I met Dani. It didn't take her long to convince me she was the one thing I'd always been searching for."

"If I had a woman like Dani who loved me, I might feel the same." Or maybe not. Bull riding had been his life for years.

"You might have to give yourself a chance to fall in love," Pierce said.

"Maybe I will." He couldn't deny that Sydney was getting to him, but she was firmly planted in her career. He couldn't see her giving that up to follow a bull rider from town to town.

"I better get back to the house," he said. "Sydney will be ready to roll again. It almost killed her to take time out from the investigation long enough to change out of her bloody clothes."

"Understandable and admirable," Pierce said. He clapped Tucker between the shoulders—a man's hug when they were afraid a real hug would let too many of those pesky emotions escape.

"I'm available to talk about anything if you want to toss possibilities around. I can't tell you what to do, though. That has to come from inside yourself."

"Same here," Pierce said. "Whatever you decide, I'll back you fully and put you to work on the ranch while you're deciding what to do next."

Both were as supportive as Tucker had expected. He was as undecided as ever, but being with Sydney and seeing what she was up against had left him with no time or energy for courting the blues.

"We'll talk more later," he said, turning to go.

"Do you mind if I call Dani and give her a heads-up on why Sydney is really in town?"

"No. It's out in the open now. If you miss anything, Sydney will fill her in when we get there."

"Be careful out there, bro," Pierce called.

That was number two on his agenda. Number one was keeping Sydney safe.

THE BELL ABOVE the door tinkled as Sydney and Tucker stepped inside Dani's Delights. The place was far more crowded than it had been yesterday. Tables had been pushed together on the left side of the room, accommodating at least a dozen women.

Most looked to be in their fifties and sixties and they were all talking and laughing at once and sipping whipped-cream-topped iced lattes. The rest of the crowd was a mixed bag of people—all ages, both genders, most in shorts or jeans, a few in suits.

When Dani spotted Sydney and Tucker, she untied her ruffled white apron and waved them to the counter where she was finishing up with a customer.

"I have everything you ordered, Mrs. Miles, and tell your husband I put a complimentary oatmeal-raisin cookie right out of the oven in there for him."

"Thank you. That's Dudley's favorite."

"I know. He checks in to see if I have them a couple of times a week."

Sydney stared at the rail-thin woman Dani was talking to. That had to be Angela Miles's mother. Only with her pale complexion and the deep wrinkles around her mouth and eyes, she looked years older than Sydney would have expected.

She took her package of pastries from Dani and walked out of the shop looking straight ahead as if avoiding eye contact with anyone in the crowded shop.

Sydney couldn't help but feel sorry for her. It surely broke her heart to lose her grandson so tragically, and then lose her daughter to the bars of a prison cell.

Tucker sidled up to the counter. "Hate to interrupt business, Dani, but can you spare a few minutes to talk? It's important."

"I'll make time. Tammy can handle things for me."

The young woman who was boxing giant cinnamon rolls dripping with creamy frosting assured her she could.

"We can talk in my office behind the kitchen," Dani said. "It's small but a little quieter than it is in here. Plus we'll have some privacy."

"Perfect." Sydney joined Dani behind the

counter. It was obvious Dani had talked to Riley, which meant one less painful explanation Sydney would have to give concerning Rachel and the investigation.

They followed Dani through the spacious kitchen with its giant ovens and long, wide counters for rolling out dough and mixing batter. The equipment and tools of the trade that were in plain sight were all shiny and sparkling clean.

Dani perched on the corner of her desk. Sydney and Tucker took the two metal folding chairs.

"Can I get you guys some coffee? Or food?"

"We've been at Esther's," Sydney said.

Dani laughed. "Enough said. No one ever leaves there hungry."

"I suppose Riley told you my real name is Sydney Maxwell."

"He did. In fact, he did a good job of catching me up on the situation."

"I should apologize for lying to you when we met."

"No need to apologize. You had good reason. Besides, the instant bond I felt with you had nothing to do with your name. I still expect us to be friends."

"I appreciate that."

Dani stared at Sydney's bandaged hand. "Could I get you some ice or lotion or some antibiotic cream before we get started? Or something for pain? Riley said you took a bad fall this morning."

"My elbows got the worst of it. Hence the long-sleeved blouse in ninety-five-degree weather. But none of the cuts are deep. No stitches needed and Esther and Grace gave me the full first-aid treatment. I'm fine."

"If you change your mind, I have some Tylenol. I can't tell you how sorry I am to hear about your sister. I became positively ill when Riley told me."

"It's not been easy," Sydney admitted. "I just have to think positive and stay focused on finding her. That's the reason I stopped by your bakery yesterday."

"So," Riley said, "do you have a photo?"

"I do." Sydney slipped Rachel's photograph from the inside pocket of her handbag and handed it to Dani. "Do you remember seeing her? She was in here on Saturday, September 14, around two fifteen."

Dani scrutinized the picture for several seconds before responding. "She was in here. I remember because she was interested in the same pottery collection you asked about. She bought one of my favorite pieces, an odd-shaped bowl in a terra-cotta glaze."

"Was she with anyone?"

"Not that I remember, but I can't say for sure. I don't even remember if she sat down or if she picked up something to go. We were particularly busy that Saturday. Several of the stores had sidewalk sales to get rid of their summer items."

"Do you remember if Rachel mentioned anything about going to a resort in Austin?"

Dani shook her head. "I'm drawing a blank. If she mentioned it, I don't remember."

Frustration swelled again. Sydney couldn't bear another dead end.

"What about film from your security camera?" Tucker asked. "How long do you keep that?"

"At least a month or two."

"Then you must have it for September 14."

"I had it until this morning when Sheriff Cavazos came in and asked for all my tapes. I gave them to him. I had no idea at the time that you needed them."

"Not a problem," Sydney assured her. "If

there's anything of use in them, I'm sure I can get access." Through proper channels or around them.

"If it matters, he didn't just request mine," Dani said. "One of the women who works part-time at the candle shop came in for a scone right after the sheriff left here and she said he'd requested theirs, as well."

"Even better. Did Riley mention that the fall that led to my discovering Rachel's car this morning was in the same area where Angela Miles's son's body was found?"

"He did. That's bizarre but I can't imagine the two can be connected in any way. You know, I moved here and bought this bakery to have a safe place to raise my niece. I'm beginning to have doubts about the safety factor."

"Was that Angela Miles's mother you were waiting on when we came in?"

"Yes, it was. Poor woman. She's become a shadow of the woman she was before her grandson died. She used to come in and talk to everybody. Now she barely speaks to me."

"I'm sure she's heartbroken," Sydney said.

"I'm sure, but her daughter is a very sick young woman. I just hope she's finally getting the psychiatric help she needs."

Sydney and Tucker had thanked Dani for her help and had just stepped out of the shop and back into the blistering sun when Sydney's phone rang.

"Hello, Jackson."

"I'm glad I caught you," he said. "Are you by yourself?"

"No. Tucker is with me."

"Glad to hear that. I have bad news."

Chapter Ten

Sydney's fingers tightened around the phone, bracing herself as best she could for Jackson's news.

"What is it?"

"We weren't able to get any usable fingerprints from the exterior of Rachel's car."

Sydney exhaled sharply, releasing the breath she hadn't realized she was holding. A fingerprint report was the least of what she'd been dreading, but she knew from his tone there was more.

"And inside the SUV?" she asked.

"We retrieved several different fingerprints. I'm sorry to have to hit you with this, but the prints of one of the missing women was found inside the car."

The ray of hope she'd held on to that Rachel might not be one of the serial abductor's victims disintegrated. She was disheartened, but not surprised. On some level of consciousness, she'd known that all along.

"Whose prints were they?"

"Michelle Dickens."

Sydney had always had a keen short-term memory for relevant facts. She reviewed in her mind what she'd learned about Michelle at her meeting with Jackson's team yesterday. Age twenty-five. Disappeared after leaving a friend's parent's vacation cabin near Winding Creek.

Michelle had spent two days there reuniting with a group of sorority friends from University of Texas. Attractive. Brunette as all the missing women were. Had no police record. Currently working as a petroleum engineer.

"Are you okay?" Jackson asked.

"I'm getting there. I was just trying to remember what I know about Michelle."

"We have more information on her today than yesterday—on Michelle and the others. What's the chance you can come by the cabin today?"

"Chances are always excellent if you have relevant facts. What time?"

"I'm available now, but I can make an appointment for later if that suits your schedule better."

"Now works."

"Will you be bringing Tucker Lawrence with you?"

"Will it be a problem if I do?"

"No. In fact, I'd welcome him."

She hadn't been expecting that response though the two men had seemed to bond at the wrecked car scene that morning.

"Any particular reason why you want him there?" she asked.

"He knows his way around the back roads and the rural areas and he has excellent connections in his brothers, who live here, his sister-in-law who owns the bakery and Esther Kavanaugh, who, according to Sheriff Cavazos, knows everyone around these parts. And except for a few speeding tickets, he's whistle clean. And I'm assuming he told you he's a championship bull rider. How's that for tough?"

Tough and thoughtful. Those two didn't always come in the same package. "Sounds like you ran a background check on him?"

"Of course. Don't worry. He checked out.

Plus we won't be discussing anything that's classified. Did Dani remember seeing Rachel in the bakery?"

"She did, even remembered selling her a piece of pottery. She didn't remember if Rachel had been alone."

"I expect that information to be forthcoming. We'll talk more when you get here."

"Thanks for calling," she said. "One or both of us will see you in a few minutes."

"Who are we going to see in a few minutes?" Tucker asked when she broke the connection.

"Jackson Clark, but you don't have to go. I can handle this and I'm sure your brothers and Esther would enjoy some time with you."

"There you go, trying to get rid of me again."

"You're a glutton for punishment."

"Right. Ask any bull who's ever sent me flying into the dirt. You mentioned fingerprints and someone named Michelle. What's that about?"

"Michelle Dickens. She's one of the women who went missing a couple of months before Rachel did. They found her fingerprints inside Rachel's car."

"Son of a bitch." Tucker took her arm. "Excuse the outburst, but I know that finding out for certain she was abducted wasn't the news you were hoping for. Not the news I was hoping for, either. But in a way it's good news. It means the abductor kept Michelle alive for at least two months."

"Yes, but living under the control of a madman."

Tucker put an arm around her waist and started to his truck.

She stopped walking. "I need to take my own car this time before it gets labeled abandoned and towed to the pound."

"I'm not even sure they have a lot for impounding cars in Winding Creek. But even if they do, you don't have to worry. By nightfall, everyone in Winding Creek will know it's your car if they don't know it already."

"I don't see how."

"The small-town grapevine. Rumors fly at the speed of light. But if you want to take your car, I'll leave my truck here and ride with you."

"I find it hard to believe you're volunteering to become even further involved with me in this investigation."

"I'll be as involved as you'll let me be."

She should ask why, but she wasn't certain she wanted to go there again just yet. His answer might be as ambiguous as hers would be if asked why she liked having him around. All she knew was it felt right and that was good enough for now.

"We can go in your truck," she said. "My rental car is not a four-wheel drive made for back roads like the one to Jackson's cabin or whatever shortcuts you may take to Dudley Miles's ranch."

"Are you certain that's how you want to spend a chunk of your afternoon? Dudley's one of the good guys. Always has been."

"That doesn't mean all his friends, employees and acquaintances are. He may know something and not even realize he knows it."

"Do you want me to call and make sure he'll be home?"

"No. I prefer the element of surprise."

"Your game. Your call."

"Then let's go," she said. Her game was deadly, and the clock might be running out.

Jackson was the only one present when Sydney and Tucker arrived at the cabin. He wasted no time in getting down to business, leading them back to the kitchen after a quick greeting.

Sydney knew he was well aware that finding Michelle Dickens's fingerprints in Rachel's car had shot the urgency level to the moon. The women might all be saved if they could track down the kidnapper fast enough. Every second counted.

"I see your left hand is bandaged. Did you get those wounds on your elbow taken care of, too?" Jackson asked.

"They're fine. Just scratches. Esther and Dani's sister-in-law, Grace, took good care of me."

"Nice to have in-house medical care, but you need to watch for infection."

"I will. No time for complications."

"Soft drinks in the fridge, coffee in the pot," Jackson said. "Unhealthy snacks on the counter. Help yourself."

Sydney went to the fridge for a diet soda. The fridge's contents consisted of Cokes, beer and a jar of salsa. "Is this what you're living on?" Sydney asked.

"Not entirely. Rene picked up some greasy burgers and brought them over for dinner last night, and I stopped for tacos at a drive-through after we finally finished at the car scene this morning."

Sydney sat down between the two men. Pens, notepads, files, a laptop and a portable printer had been shoved to the other end of the table, no doubt to make room for Sydney and Tucker.

"I also stopped by Dani's Delights," Jackson said.

"That's odd. Tucker and I just left there and Dani didn't mention meeting you."

"I didn't introduce myself. I wanted to be sure you'd had a chance to explain about Rachel first. And I wanted to get a feel for the place before anyone realized I was FBI."

"What did you think?"

"Busy. Lots of local people who knew each other. Not a place I'd expect a serial abductor to pick out his victims, but you never know. Some of the worst have proved to be a Prince Charming until the full truth came out."

"An abductor and likely a killer," Sydney corrected.

"Alleged killer," Jackson said. "The deeper I get into this, the less convinced I am that Sara Goodwin's killing is related to the disappearance of the others. She doesn't seem to match the pattern."

"In what way?" Tucker asked.

"She was sixteen and homeless. Didn't have a car. The only tie to Winding Creek is that her body was found near here. The others were between the ages of twenty-five and thirty-two and all appeared to be in this area by choice. And at this point, they are only missing."

"Has at least one of our agents interviewed the friends and/or relatives of all the missing women?"

"No, but we're making progress. Rene's at the airport now, taking the short flight to Shreveport to meet with Alice Baker's roommate. He won't be back until late tonight. I'll shoot that report to you as soon as he gets it to me."

"Thanks. Do you have any additional information from the Shreveport Police Department?"

"I just got off the phone with a detective who has talked to the roommate twice. He says her story hasn't changed, so he has nothing new to add to his report."

"Then the printouts and digital files you gave me yesterday are up to date on Alice Baker?"

"It's all I have until we hear from Rene. Tim did an in-depth interview with Michelle Dickens's parents this morning, but he's driving back to San Antonio to give them the latest news in person."

"What about Karen Murphy?" Sydney prodded.

"Next on the list. Her truck-driver husband will be home from his cross-country run later tonight, and Tim and I will be interviewing him first thing in the morning at their home in New Braunfels. That is unless a more pressing matter takes precedence, such as we had when you discovered Rachel's car this morning."

Jackson picked up a folder filled with handwritten notes torn from small notebooks. He shoved it across the table to Sydney. "These are copies of the notes the guys scribbled down yesterday during their research and interviews. I'd like you to do the same with your impressions from visiting the crime scene this morning. I want to keep us all on the same page."

"Sometimes hastily scribbled notes are more useful than the formal reports," Sydney said. "Off-the-cuff comments cut to the chase." Sydney opened the folder. There were two sets of notes, carefully stapled together.

She picked up the top one. Michelle Dickens, age 25, missing since August 20.

Michelle was a kindergarten teacher in Kerrville, Texas, who was engaged to be married the first week in October. Got along with everyone. Athletic. Loved hiking, biking, rock climbing and snow skiing.

She was last seen at her parents' house before driving back to Kerrville after spending the weekend shopping for a wedding dress. She didn't buy one. Paper trail ended with a charge made at an Exxon station on the highway about ten miles from Winding Creek. Parents in state of almost-crippling panic.

Sydney understood that completely. She looked through the next set of notes. Alice Baker. Lived in Shreveport, Louisiana, with her roommate. An unemployed petroleum engineer, she had been traveling to San Antonio on March 9 for a job interview. She'd never kept the appointment.

She had charged a pair of Western boots at a boutique in Winding Creek and food and drinks at Caffe's Bar and Grill.

Her roommate insisted she was extremely

cautious, not the kind to even talk to strangers, much less get in the car with one. Alice was licensed to carry and always packed a small pistol when she traveled alone.

Obviously, she hadn't seen trouble coming in time to use her weapon. Or if she'd hesitated to pull the trigger, the perp might have wrestled it away from her. That happened far too often with inexperienced shooters.

"Our perp is definitely not straying far from his community playground," Sydney commented. "He doesn't necessarily live here, but he spends a lot of time here."

"If he sticks this close to home, he's either extremely brazen or thinks he's too smart to get caught," Jackson said.

"Or he wants to get caught," Sydney said.

"I plan to oblige him," Jackson said. "I'm still puzzled by how and why he drove the car into the ravine. I can't imagine he trusted Michelle to drive Rachel's car while he followed her in his. Too much opportunity for her to escape."

"Unless she's experiencing the Stockholm syndrome and has bonded with the kidnapper," Sydney said. "If that's the situation, she might be helping him kidnap the others."

Sydney was almost certain that Rachel would never let herself be brainwashed by her kidnapper. But she couldn't be positive of that.

"You're in cowboy country," Tucker said. "First thing I thought of was horses. The second was four-wheelers. Almost every ranch has those."

"If he had someone follow them on horseback, that would mean he has an accomplice."

"Not necessarily," Tucker said. "Based on the assumption he is local and holding the women nearby, he could have hauled a couple of horses up in a trailer. Same with an ATV. I noticed the SUV had a trailer hitch."

"I missed that," Sydney said, hating to admit she'd overlooked any detail. "But I would have seen a trailer if there had been one."

"He could have come back for that later, in his car or whatever he drives."

"Just thinking," Jackson said, "but why bring the girl along at all if she wasn't driving the SUV for him?"

"Maybe he was afraid she'd escape if he left her behind," Tucker said.

"No, if he's holding her prisoner, he has a way to keep her imprisoned," Sydney said.

"But maybe he wanted her to think he was taking her out to kill her and leave her body to rot in the woods."

Or maybe he had done exactly that and the body hadn't been found yet. Her insides quaked at that possibility.

"Dani said Sheriff Cavazos requested film from her security cameras this morning. Were you aware of that?"

"I am. He'd already pulled several places in town as part of his ongoing investigation. He's sending us copies of those as well as film from several other shops, restaurants and bars that he's collecting today. The locals trust him, so they're cooperating fully. They also want that perp found. The natives are definitely getting restless and with good reason."

"When will you get the film?" Sydney asked.

"Cavazos said by late afternoon. Then I'll shoot it to Lane and have him work his analysis magic."

"Let me know when you get that."

"Believe me, I will. And if you come up with any kind of theory as to the identity of the perp, you are to get back to me at once. No going after him alone. Get that?"

"Of course."

"*Not* the way you did with the Swamp Strangler."

"Trust me. I will never make that mistake again."

She finished her drink and carried the empty can to the trash basket.

"Where do you go from here?" Jackson asked.

"To pay a call on Dudley and Millie Miles. You must agree with me that it's extremely coincidental that Rachel's car was dumped in almost the exact spot where the Mileses' grandson's body was dumped."

"I agree, but I talked to the sheriff and one of his deputies about Dudley Miles. Neither of them could say enough good things about the man. His daughter was another story—narcissistic with no sense of decency—but she's in prison."

"I told her the same thing," Tucker said.

"I believe both of you. I just want to talk to the man. He must have a lot of cowboys running the ranch. He can talk to them and see if any of them came into contact with Rachel. The perp we're looking for might even be one of his workers. We have no reason to weed out that possibility."

"You're right. Go with your instincts. Just get me a profile on the perp that leads us to him before he strikes again."

"I plan to do just that."

Hopefully talking to Dudley Miles would help that along.

Chapter Eleven

They stopped for a late lunch at Hank's. The smell of hot grease, onions and spices made her nauseous. She knew it was more nerves than odors, but the only remedy she knew for that was to keep at it.

She spent most of her time there showing Rachel's photograph to the few waitresses she'd missed the last time she was here and to some of the customers Hank pointed out as regulars who might have seen Rachel either in his place or around town.

People were sympathetic and took a good look at the picture. Again, no luck.

They left as soon as Tucker finished his burger. Her grilled chicken salad was untouched except for moving a few greens around with her fork.

She fought to keep the dark and frightening thoughts at bay. All her energy was needed to keep her focus sharp and driving. They were ten minutes into the drive before she noticed that Tucker was wearing the now-familiar brooding expression of a troubled man.

As depressing as the situation was that she'd dragged him into, she knew that was not the only thing he was dealing with. She'd noticed that the first night they'd talked, even before she'd interrupted his whiskey and gloom.

"I get the feeling you have something other than this investigation on your mind. Do you want to talk about it?"

"Am I that obvious?"

"No, I'm that intuitive."

"Which is no doubt why you're a great profiler. I have some decisions I need to make. Nothing nearly as critical or urgent as what you're dealing with, so let's not get into it today."

His phone rang before she had time to delve deeper. He punched the answer button on his dashboard. A second later, Esther's voice filled the car.

"I hope I didn't catch you at a bad time. Are you still with Sydney?"

"I am. We're in my truck and my phone is on Speaker. What's on your mind?"

"I know how important it is for you to be with Sydney right now, but I just got off the phone with Dani. She says Constance wants to know when she's going to see her uncle Tucker."

"I'd like to spend some time with her and Jaci. Maybe tonight."

"That's why I'm calling. We're talking about having a family dinner tonight. Nothing fancy, just a few of your favorites. Fried chicken. Fresh peas from the garden."

"You do know how to lure me in. Throw in a banana pudding and I'm there."

"Banana pudding is a given when you're in town."

"I'm not exactly sure what time we'll get back there, so don't make it before seven."

"You'll come, too, won't you, Sydney?" Esther asked.

"I think it's best if I don't. I would only be a drag on the party atmosphere."

"Everyone understands what you're going through, so they won't be expecting frivolity or bubbly from you. And you can meet my two adorable granddaughters."

"I'd love to meet them."

"And you have to eat to keep up your energy. So it's settled?"

"Settled," she agreed. "I have to work tonight, but I'll make time for dinner."

A boisterous, loving family was probably not what she needed right now. But they had all done so much for Sydney, she could hardly say no, especially knowing it would mean so much to Esther.

After Tucker broke the connection, he reached for her hand and gave it a squeeze. "I won't let them hold you to the dinner promise if you're not up to it."

She hadn't stopped to think that he might not want her there, throwing a damper on the gathering with his family. He was giving her his days. He might well want his nights to himself. She wondered again about the decisions he was making and if they involved a woman.

"When you said work, you didn't mean you're planning to go out trolling for the perp alone, did you?" Tucker asked. "Because if you are, I need to call Esther right now and cancel my dinner plans."

"No," she said. "I'll be working at the

ranch, but you can't follow me around forever, Tucker. You must have bulls waiting."

"The bulls and I are taking a break."

She wasn't sure what that meant, but she went back to watching the pastoral scenes fly by as the road became hillier. She was certain she'd never seen this many cows, bulls and horses in her life.

They passed a huge red barn on the east side of the road that she was certain she'd seen before. The land to the west of them was fenced with barbwire but heavily wooded. "Is this where we were this morning?"

"If we turned down the next dirt imitation of a road we come to and followed to the top of the waterfall we'd end up in the same exact spot. Another mile down this road and we'll arrive at Dudley's spread."

"Then it would be possible for the perp and Michelle to have driven the car to the waterfall and then ridden horses or an all-terrain vehicle back to land belonging to Dudley Miles without ever getting on anything except dirt roads."

"It's possible," Tucker admitted. "It's also possible they rode west into an area of dozens of small farms and weekend ranches owned by people who like to get out of town and experience the country lifestyle when they can."

"I strongly suspect Sheriff Cavazos checked all those out before he requested help from the FBI."

"He's likely checked out Dudley's wranglers, as well."

"I'll still feel better after I meet Dudley Miles for myself."

The wooded area gave way to lush green rolling hills and a seemingly unending strand of white-painted farm fencing that had cost someone a small fortune.

Tucker pulled up and stopped in front of a magnificent double-arched black iron gate. Two huge black ironwork stallions were built into the fence, their front feet reared up as if they were about to attack each other. Their heads and long necks extended over the top edge of the gate. Two brick columns supported the gate.

"I don't think I've ever seen a gate that impressive," Sydney said. "It's like a piece of expensive art."

"I'm sure it cost like one, too." Tucker lowered his window, reached out and punched a button on the brick support post. The gate swung open.

"I'm surprised it wasn't locked," Sydney said.

"No one does a lot of locking gates around here. Never needed to until now. I suspect that might change if an arrest is not made soon."

Once the gate had closed behind them, Tucker made a call to Dudley to let him know he had company.

"Tucker Lawrence. I heard you were in town. Glad you found time to stop by and see me. I'm out checking on the hay baling, so you'll have to give me a few minutes to get back to the house."

"No problem."

"Wait on the porch if you don't mind. Millie's usually napping this time of day. Better not to wake her."

Tucker made a couple of turns on a winding road before the house came into view. It was a far cry from what she'd expected. "Wow! We're not in Kansas anymore. I'm not even sure we're in Texas. Who knew ranchers lived like this?"

"I CAN ASSURE you that most don't," Tucker said as he climbed from the truck and hurried over to open her door. "The most popular rumor is that Millie Miles got stuck in the pages of *Gone with the Wind* and never escaped."

"She has all the antebellum trappings. Second-and third-floor wraparound verandas. Wide, winding staircase. Huge white columns. Beautiful garden. All she needs is Rhett Butler."

"She doesn't need him. She has a cowboy," Tucker teased. "To set the record straight, that is never settling for less."

"You could be biased. I'll reserve judgment until I've met the man," Sydney said.

They took the paved walk to the steps. He put a hand to the small of her back as they climbed the stairs to the shaded veranda. Once there, Sydney settled into a cushioned rocker. Tucker propped against one of the support columns.

It had been several years since Tucker had been to the Eagle's Nest Ranch and he'd forgotten how pretentious and out of place the house was among the rolling pastures of the Texas Hill Country.

"The first time I visited this ranch was years before I went to live with Esther and

Charlie," he said, sliding far back into his past. "I was in the first or possibly the second grade. My class made a field trip out here so that us 'town' kids could get a taste of life on a working ranch."

"Is that trip what inspired you to become a bull rider?"

"No, that came years later, when I didn't get a contract from the NFL and realized I might have to take a real job. But I had been competing in bull-riding events for years by then."

"But even as a kid, you must have been impressed with all this."

"You got it. I went home and told my mother we'd been to the White House and met the president. When she stopped laughing, she tried to convince me differently. It took a lot of explaining to persuade me I was wrong."

Sydney laughed. The sound caught him by surprise. It was the first time he'd enlisted more than a tentative smile from her. He loved hearing it, but the joy was immediately choked off by a knot of revulsion and bitterness.

His muscles bunched. If he could get to the monster who was putting Sydney, Rachel and so many others through this hell, he'd swear he could kill the man with his bare hands.

It was a brand of hatred he'd never experienced before.

Tucker heard the clopping of approaching hooves and looked up to see Dudley riding toward them on a splendid black steed. He climbed out of the saddle and tethered the animal to a low branch of a young oak tree several feet away from the porch.

Dudley grinned broadly as he climbed the stairs. His shoulders were stooped and the hair that had been almost black a few years back was almost completely gray. His ruddy, wrinkled flesh might pass for leather. The years since his grandson's tragic death had clearly not been kind to him.

Dudley extended a weathered, callused hand. "Great to see you, Tucker. You look fit, as always." The two of them shook hands before Dudley turned toward Sydney.

"And this is Sydney Maxwell. You must have heard of her by now."

"Yes. News does travel fast in Winding Creek."

Sydney extended her hand. "Nice to meet you, Mr. Miles."

He shook her hand. "Just call me Dudley. Everyone does."

"Have you talked to the sheriff lately?" Tucker asked.

"Yep. He was out earlier today, doing what he called routine questioning of some of my wranglers. It was a waste of time and I told him so. I know my men. They may not be sophisticated but they're hard workers and they're honest. Otherwise, they don't last past their first payday."

"Sometimes people can fool you," Sydney said.

"Sometimes," Dudley agreed. "But I can still assure you I don't have any perverted, murderous kidnappers working for me. Anyway, Cavazos mentioned that one of the FBI agents on this case was a sister to one of the victims and staying with Esther Kavanaugh. I reckon that's you."

"Yes. I'm hoping to find someone who might have seen my sister, Rachel, while she was in Winding Creek. Someone who would know if she was alone or seemed to be in distress. I know they're familiar with a few details of the other missing women by now, but no one has likely heard of Rachel."

"Good idea. It's nice Tucker is here to show you around the town. We don't see much of him. I suppose he told you he's a big-time bull-riding champion."

"I didn't tell it nearly as well as you just did," Tucker said.

"All you Lawrence brothers are much too modest. But to get back to the crisis at hand. Does the FBI have any suspects?"

"Not that I know of," Sydney said. "Hopefully that will change soon."

"I'd like to do something to help before you leave. What about my offering a reward for information leading to the women's rescue?"

"That's a generous offer," Tucker acknowledged.

"I like to help in cases like this when I can. Give it some thought," he added when Sydney didn't jump on the offer. "Just tell me how much you think would be appropriate and I'll write you a check."

Dudley pulled a key from his pocket, unlocked the front door and pushed it open. "C'mon in. I'm already as hot and sweaty as I can get, but no reason for the two of you to stand out here in the heat."

They followed him through the house and onto a glassed-in porch that ran the length of the back of the house. The room overlooked a kidney-shaped pool surrounded by chic outdoor furniture and huge pots of blooming plants. No beach towels in sight. No floats. Every lounge chair was perfectly straight.

Tucker wondered how long it had been since anyone had actually swum in the pool. Even the room they were in now seemed more for show than relaxing. Sydney chose a straight-back love seat. He sat down beside her.

"If you two will excuse me for a minute, I need to call Becker to come get my mount and see that he's put away properly. Then I'm going to grab myself a tall glass of iced tea. What can I bring you to drink? A beer? Cocktail? It's five o'clock somewhere."

"Iced tea sounds good," Sydney said.

"Nothing for me," Tucker said.

As soon as Dudley left the room, Sydney leaned in close. "Do you think he really meant the offer of a reward?"

"I'm sure he did. Charlie always said that if your mule was in a ditch, his best friend Dudley would be along with a tractor to pull you out, and then offer you a new mule to go with the one he'd rescued."

"He and Charlie must have been very close."

"They were. Friends from back in their

high school years. They were always there for each other."

Except Dudley obviously hadn't come rushing in with a check when Charlie was drowning in debt and about to lose the ranch and the house. Of course, Charlie was so damned independent, he'd probably never let Dudley know how bad things were.

Dudley rejoined them with the two glasses of tea in hand. He set one atop a coaster on a small mahogany table next to Sydney and took a chair opposite them.

Dudley leaned back and crossed a foot over the opposite knee. "How's the bull-riding business going, Tucker?" he asked, casually changing the subject from Rachel's disappearance as if they were here to shoot the bull.

"I've had a good year." Good enough that he could be headed to a national championship win if he could get his head on straight.

"Glad to hear that. I've caught your performances a few times on TV this year. Not often since I tend to fall asleep in my chair about ten minutes after I turn on the TV at night. The announcers can't say enough good things about you."

"I've been lucky."

"Some, but mostly you've worked hard at it. Plus you're a natural. Charlie was so proud of you and your brothers. I couldn't believe the change that came over him and Esther when you three boys moved in with them. It's a shame they couldn't have kids of their own."

"Were you and Charlie close friends?" Sydney asked.

Tucker had already had this conversation with Sydney and had no idea where she was going now.

"We didn't see that much of each other over the last few years. I wish I'd kept up with him better, but we still got together occasionally to go hunting or fishing. He was a good man. It took the heart and soul right out of Esther when he committed suicide. Only thing that saved her was having Riley and Pierce and their families move in around her."

"She believes he was murdered," Sydney said.

That explained where this was heading, but surely she didn't think there was a link between Charlie's death and Rachel's abduction.

"When I first heard the news, I thought suicide didn't seem at all like Charlie," Dudley said. "He was a man of faith and conviction and I couldn't see him leaving Esther for any reason. But he was shot with his own gun. No other fingerprints on it. No evidence that anyone had been anywhere near the barn that day but him. Sheriff Cavazos said it was obvious suicide and I had no reason to doubt him."

"Cavazos told Riley and Pierce the same thing," Tucker said. "He assured them the investigation had been thorough and there was no evidence of foul play."

Dudley sipped his tea and then licked moisture from his bottom lip. "You know, I don't think I ever told anyone this, but Charlie paid me a visit a few days before he took his life."

"Did he talk about his debt problems?"

"No. If he had I would have bailed him out. You know that. He came because he was worried about me, though he must have been horrified of losing his ranch and the only life he and Esther had ever known."

Sydney uncrossed her legs and leaned forward. "What did he tell you?"

"That he knew I was lying to protect Angela and that I would never have gotten drunk when I was supposed to be tending my grandson, that I would never have dumped his small body in the woods."

"Shows how well he knew you," Tucker said.

"He said he had proof and that if I didn't tell the truth in court, he was going to take his proof to the sheriff. Looking back, I 'spect he might have done just that if he'd stayed alive awhile longer."

"And you wouldn't have gone to prison for Angela's crime," Sydney said. "You're certain you never told anyone about this?"

"Nope. Probably shouldn't have mentioned it to you now. God knows I don't want anything said that will upset my wife any more than she already is."

"How is Millie?" Tucker asked.

"She goes through some of the motions of living, but it's like there's no heart left in her. She goes into town a couple of days a week, runs a few errands, goes to church, sometimes even has lunch with old friends.

"Crazy thing is she can't stay in the house all day yet can't stand driving. Sometimes she insists she needs one of my wranglers to drive her where she wants to go."

"Good thing you have one to spare," Tucker said. "Pierce says good help is getting hard to find."

"True. That's one reason I've never moved

any of my livestock over to that strip of land I bought from Mike Kurlacky when he got the gout so bad he couldn't take care of himself, much less his cattle."

"Is that land lying idle?"

"More or less. Millie gave one of my wranglers, Roy Sales, use of it to raise some hogs while I was in prison. He's living there now, but I'd take it back if you ever decide to settle down back here in Winding Creek and want to buy it. Plenty of room to raise some rodeo stock."

"That day might not be too far away."

"Roy did all the repairs on the house while I was in prison. Millie said she wanted to do something to pay him back. But enough of that. I know you came here to talk about more urgent stuff than hogs and cattle."

Sydney reached into her handbag and took out the photo of Rachel. "I'd appreciate it if you'd take a look at my sister's photo and tell me if you remember ever seeing her in Winding Creek."

Dudley studied the photo. "She doesn't look familiar. Unless she was hanging out at the hardware store, the feed and tack store or the saddle repair shop, it's not likely I'd have run into her."

"What I'm really hoping for is to find out who she might have been seen with before she disappeared."

"Makes sense. The abductor has to be hooking up with his victims somewhere."

"I have extra copies of the photo. I'll leave that one with you. Perhaps your wife or some of your wranglers may have seen her."

"That's a damn good idea. I'll post the photo in the bunkhouse and tell them to check it out. Now back to my offer of a reward. How about twenty-five thousand dollars for anyone who gives information that leads to the rescue of the four missing women?"

"That's extremely generous," Sydney said. "If you're serious I'll talk to my supervisor at the FBI and see how he wants to handle this."

"I'm serious as the business end of a .45."

"If that's settled, we should probably be going and let you get back to work," Tucker said.

"You're right. A rancher can't afford to be burning daylight these days." Dudley gulped down the last of his iced tea and stood.

Sydney thanked Dudley again for his cooperation and reward offer as he walked them to the front door. There was no sign of Millie.

"If you're this way in the fall, let's do some hunting, Tucker."

"I'll hold you to that if I get back this way," Tucker said. "Can't make any promises. The fall rodeo circuit doesn't allow for much time off."

But if he didn't get back to bull riding soon, he may as well spend the fall hunting. He still needed to accumulate points and earnings to get to the championship round.

They'd climbed back in his truck and were still buckling their seat belts when Sydney hit him with the next humdinger.

"I think there's a good chance Charlie Kavanaugh was murdered and that someone in the Miles family is responsible."

Chapter Twelve

"Don't look so shocked," Sydney said. "I didn't pull this out of the clouds. Dudley himself offered the motive. Charlie wasn't going to go along with his lying to the court."

"Dudley just offered you twenty-five thousand dollars. He's been a philanthropist all his life, has helped fund every charity event that takes place in this part of Texas. He'd been a friend to Charlie for years. I find it hard to see him as Charlie's killer."

"I didn't say Dudley killed him. It may have been Millie or their daughter, Angela. They wouldn't have had to do the deed themselves. They could have paid someone else. Believe me, that happens far more than most people realize."

"I wouldn't put anything past Angela, but

Dudley just admitted we were the first ones he'd ever talked to about Charlie's threat."

"His life was in a state of heartbreaking turmoil at the time. He may have forgotten or Charlie may have mentioned it to someone and it got back to Angela."

"You could be right," Tucker admitted. "But I think we're jumping tracks here. Are you trying to tie what happened to Dudley's grandson to Sara Goodwin or to Rachel's and the other women's disappearance?"

"No. Not at this point, but I can't ignore the facts. I have a sworn duty to turn this information over to someone in authority. I just wanted to alert you first."

"You do what you have to do," Tucker said. "If Charlie was murdered, the last thing I want is to see his killer go free."

"Then we're on the same page."

She breathed easier. Nothing Tucker said would keep her from following her conscience but she didn't want him to feel as if she were turning on him.

She benefited from bouncing ideas off him, respected his opinion. She liked riding with him in his truck. Liked the sound of his voice and the saunter when he walked.

Sydney took a deep breath. There was no denying the swelling attraction but she couldn't deal with any of that right now. There was far too much at stake.

She was making a phone call to Jackson when they passed a lopsided gate with a crooked sign that said Kurlacky's Acres. She wondered if Tucker was serious about buying that land. From bull riding to raising bulls. Somehow she couldn't see that happening any more than she could see herself walking away from the FBI. One day maybe, but not anytime soon.

When Jackson answered, she explained Dudley's offer of the reward. As expected, he was all for it.

He had good news, as well. One of Cavazos's deputies would be dropping off a thumb drive for her at the ranch. The material would include a copy of relevant footage from Dani's Delights security camera.

She broke the connection and twisted in her seat so that she could face Tucker while she caught him up to date. He was staring straight ahead, his hands wrapped tight around the steering wheel. His brows furrowed into deep wrinkles.

"You're doing it again," she said.

"Doing what?"

"Shutting me out of what's bothering you."

"What's bothering me is that we haven't located your sister or apprehended the kidnapper from hell."

"You mentioned before that you were dealing with troubling decisions."

"It's nothing."

She didn't believe him, but then, she knew so little about him that she could be reading this all wrong. "I'm a good listener, but if you really want me to butt out, just say so and I won't mention it again."

"Is that straight from the 'good cop' manual?"

"I'll take that comment to mean you don't need my input."

They rode in silence until he turned onto Main Street for Sydney to get her car.

"I have to pick up some supplies at the drugstore before I drive back to the ranch," she said.

He nodded but didn't turn to face her until he pulled up next to her car. "Sorry for the bite of sarcasm back there. That was my macho defenses kicking in."

"Apology accepted."

"If you're still game to have me unload on you, I have a proposition for you."

He sounded so serious she was almost afraid to answer. "Let's hear it."

"Go horseback riding with me when we get back to the ranch. I know the perfect spot for you to unwind and me to spout my problems. It comes with a sunset and a fabulous view."

"Okay, cowboy. You've got yourself a deal."

IT HAD BEEN several years since Sydney had been on a horse but it took only a few minutes for her to feel at home in the saddle again. Her mount was a gentle black quarter horse named Beauty, said to be one of Constance's favorites.

Beauty needed little guidance from Sydney but easily kept up with the much-larger sorrel that Tucker rode. They started out at a walk.

"You look like you've been riding all your life," Tucker said. "You didn't mention you were such an experienced horsewoman."

"Beauty is making this easy. I dated a guy whose father owned a ranch back in college but I haven't done much riding since."

"He taught you well. Are you more comfortable at a walk or are you ready to pick up the pace a bit?"

She wanted to race like the wind, wanted to feel the wind in her face and feel as free as she had before her sister had been swallowed up by evil.

That wasn't going to happen, but losing control and being thrown by Beauty was a distinct possibility if she became too carried away. She'd already had one fall today and lucked out with only minor injuries. No reason to push her good fortune.

"Let me get used to the walk for a few more minutes. If Beauty hasn't turned on me by then, we can move up to an easy lope."

"A lope. You're starting to sound like a cowgirl."

"You know the old saying. Love a horse before you fall in love with a man."

"And did you?"

"Fall in love with the horse or a man?"

"Either."

"Not yet, but I could quickly grow fond of a sweet little filly like Beauty."

Tucker picked up the pace and she followed a few paces behind. He sat straight in the saddle, his long legs a perfect fit in the stirrups, his Stetson making the definitive statement. This was his world. Livestock, horses, bull riding. He was the real deal.

Tucker slowed until they were riding side by side. He looked at her and tipped his hat. Something bubbled inside her like fine champagne. Her pulse quickened.

"You're smiling," he said. "Does that mean you're up for a longer ride?"

"Sure. My overwrought nerves are even starting to unknot a bit." At least for the moment.

"Then let's take the horses to a gallop and see if the ranching spirit can refresh your soul."

She experienced a full five minutes of exhilaration before a new wave of anxiety and guilt hit with the force of exploding dynamite. Her fingers tangled in Beauty's reins as horrifying images swept through her mind.

Rachel, enduring the touch of a monster. Rachel, starving and begging for food. Rachel, cowering in fear while she prayed and waited in vain for her FBI agent sister to come to her rescue.

It took all Sydney's mental strength to keep

the images from sinking into the blackest pit of all.

She took deep breaths, fighting to return to full mental control. Guilt and panic were two of the worst possible emotions for her in this situation. *Undue stress leads to poor decision-making.* She'd heard that countless times since coming to work for the Bureau.

She wasn't in this alone. Jackson and three of the top agents in the FBI were working this case. Local law enforcement with all their manpower were out there hitting the streets day and night.

An hour's time spent with Tucker after a day that started at daybreak would only make her more alert, more focused and better able to give Jackson what he needed from her.

An accurate profile of the perp so that they could narrow their parameters and track him down before he struck again or a new body was discovered.

She straightened in the saddle and took a deep breath. In minutes, she'd talked herself through the panic attack. Her nerves settled enough that she could appreciate the serenity of the environment.

They had obviously been steadily climbing while she'd been overcome with her bout of needless guilt. They were at the crest of a hill. Acres and acres of rolling pastures criss-crossed by barbwire and dotted with clusters of towering pines and ancient oaks stretched out in all directions.

The sky above was painted in streams of gold as the sun began its descent to the distant horizon. She reined in Beauty to a slow walk and let the tranquility seep bone-deep.

Tucker came back to join her. "This is the best view on the ranch."

"It's amazing, like a painting springing to life as I watch."

"When I was twelve, I used to ride up here and pretend I was the king and all the land I could see was my kingdom."

"I suppose it is someone's kingdom. Is this all part of the Double K?"

"Not all, but a good bit of it. Charlie bought it when land was cheap. A spread like this today would cost like it was a rich kingdom. Esther sold it to Pierce for a fraction of its true worth."

"Did it upset you and Riley that she chose to sell it to Pierce?"

"Not in the least. A ranch this size is an

enormous amount of work and responsibility. Riley and I weren't ready to take that on and likely never will be. It all worked out great. Pierce is a born rancher. Esther will always have her home. It's a win-win."

Tucker dismounted and then helped her from the saddle. He tethered their horses to a tree branch near a shallow creek. Both horses quickly waded in and lowered their necks for a long drink.

"There's more to see," Tucker said, "though you might prefer to miss it."

"Why would I?"

"It's another rocky gorge, steeper than this morning but with far less water rushing over the edge to the rocky creek below."

"Since we've already proved I'm about as graceful and sure-footed as a drunk chimp on skates, how about we save that for next time?"

"The next time it is."

Tucker took a small Mexican blanket from his saddlebag and tossed it over his shoulder. They walked upstream a few yards before he spread the blanket over a thick carpet of grass and pine straw.

Sydney knelt and then settled herself cross-legged.

Tucker joined her on the blanket except that he stretched out on his back and tugged his Stetson low on his forehead to protect from the glare of the low-riding sun.

A honeyed warmth crept through her. Wrong time. Wrong place. But being with Tucker felt so right.

"I can tell you're good at it, but what made you choose a career with the FBI?" Tucker asked.

"My dad was a homicide detective. He was the most amazing and bravest man I knew and I always wanted to follow in his footsteps. He raised Rachel and me pretty much single-handedly after my mother died from complications from what was supposed to be routine removal of a benign tumor."

"Where is your dad now?"

"He died of a bullet wound to the head trying to intervene and save a kid who'd gotten caught up in gang warfare. He had one more year until he retired."

"How old were you then?"

"It was my first year in college. When I graduated, I was hired by the FBI and knew from day one it was where I belonged."

"You picked a dangerous career."

"I try not to think too much about that. I know it involves risk, but I'm doing what I love. What's life if you lose your passion?"

"I suppose that's a question everyone has to answer at one time or another."

She untwisted her legs and lay back on her side facing him, suddenly craving the extra closeness. "Most of the time I think I have it all figured out. This week I'm hanging on by a thread that's on the verge of splitting in two. Any bravado I manage to exhibit is fake."

"That's why I'm hanging around," Tucker said. He propped himself up on his elbow so that they were inches apart and facing each other. "I'll be there to catch you if the thread snaps."

"I appreciate that, but you know that if we compared job risks, you'd win by a landslide. Bull riding has to be the most dangerous sport in the world."

"Most bull riders would agree with you on that."

"How often do you get hurt?"

"Every time I get thrown, but there are lots of different degrees of hurt. Mostly it's lumps and bruises that a six-pack of beer and a few painkillers can handle. But I've broken a few bones. Had a couple of concussions. Wounded my pride more times than I can count."

"And yet you still do it?"

"Yeah. Like you said. It's the passion. And it's my life."

"We came up here to talk about you," she said. "Lest we get sidetracked, what kind of decisions are you struggling with?"

"None," he said. "The decisions have all been made. Passion wins."

His voice grew husky. She met his gaze and felt as if she was drowning in the depths of his sun-kissed eyes.

She should move away. She should get up.

She did neither.

Tucker slipped his arms around her and pulled her close. His raw strength made her feel weak and empowered at the same time. An unfamiliar hunger raged inside her.

His lips found hers and she melted into his kiss. The world tilted out of focus, releasing a rush of mystifying emotions that created a need she couldn't fight.

Out of breath and with tears spilling from her eyes, she finally pulled away.

Tucker wiped a tear from her cheek with the back of his hand. "I'm so sorry, Sydney.

I don't know what came over me. It just happened and then..."

"Please don't be sorry. I'm not crying because you kissed me. I don't even know why I'm crying. It's just that I'm an emotional wreck and I just can't do this right now."

"I understand. Just know that I never meant to hurt you or take advantage of your vulnerability. That's the last thing I'd willingly do."

He stood and then took her outstretched hands and pulled her to her feet.

The strength in his arms and hands almost sent her into tears again. He was her haven in the storm, but was it only safety she'd been thinking about when she got lost in his kiss?

"Promise me something," she said as they walked back to the horses.

"Anything."

"When this is over and Rachel and the others are safe, promise me we'll get together and finish that kiss."

"You've got yourself a deal."

RACHEL HEARD THE approaching footsteps but didn't cower in fear. The monster was like an attack dog. If he sensed fear, he became even more abusive and punishing.

She was experimenting with a new defense theory, a version of reverse Stockholm syndrome. Play with his mind. Give him reasons to think she understood him and enjoyed his horrid visits to her private hellhole.

The door opened. She forced a smile so fake it made her sick to her stomach. "You're here," she murmured. "I was afraid something had happened to you."

"You needn't worry about that. I'm in complete control and I have a nice surprise for you."

"I hope it's that you'll take me out of this room. I can cook dinner for you while you relax."

"No—guess again. Wait. Don't bother. I'll tell you." He smiled, showing his snuff-stained teeth, and walked nearer.

"I saw your sister today."

Chapter Thirteen

There was no way of knowing if the monster was lying or telling the truth. Sometimes she wasn't even sure he knew, but there was a good chance he'd run into Sydney.

Rachel had known all along that Sydney would come looking for her as soon as she realized Rachel was missing. With FBI capabilities on her side, she'd have had no trouble following the paper trail to Winding Creek.

The monster set the plate of beans he was holding on the floor by the door. "Why so quiet? I know you're not surprised. You must be as excited as I am about having FBI Sydney join us here in our cozy home."

Say the right thing. Don't give up the game. Stay alive until Sydney and the rest of the FBI agents come storming in.

"You'd like Sydney. She's smart like you are. She figures things out that no one else can."

"If she were smart, she wouldn't be strutting around town drawing so much attention to herself. She's making this so easy on me. So ridiculously easy."

"How is she drawing attention?"

"Showing your picture to everyone she sees. Asking about you everywhere she goes. Big FBI star, coming to save you." He laughed as if that were a marvelous joke.

"Maybe you should give yourself up to Sydney and the FBI. I'll tell her you didn't really hold me captive, swear my stay here was voluntary. They couldn't do anything to you if I did that. You could go back to your life. I could go back to mine."

"You don't know what's going on here, Rachel. For an attorney, you can't figure anything out. I'll save myself. I'm the smart one."

"Don't make Sydney come after you. She never loses. Do you know what she did to the Swamp Strangler?"

"This ain't no swamp, and if I were you, I wouldn't be holding my breath waiting on her to ride to the rescue. She's picked up a cowboy to keep her company. Moved in with him, so I understand."

Rachel was certain he was lying about that. If Sydney was with a cowboy, it was because he fit into her investigation.

"Have you ever watched someone die, Rachel?"

Once again the monster's mood had changed in an instant, as if he'd traveled to some dark, Satan-held corner of his mind.

"Yes," she said honestly.

She'd arrived at the hospital just in time to see her father draw his last breath after being shot in the line of duty. Shot by someone as evil as the monster.

"One minute you're laughing while they beg you not to hurt them. The next they're choking on their own blood, terror swimming in their eyes."

He was totally in the dark zone now, making no sense, his eyes glazed over.

"How many people have you killed?" she asked softly.

"Only the ones Mommy tells me to. I'm a good boy."

A sickening terror crawled inside her. He was stark, raving mad.

Sydney was the only hope for her and for others who might be imprisoned with her. But the monster had obviously crossed the line to total insanity. At any moment, it could be too late.

ONE OF PIERCE'S newly hired wranglers was in the horse barn pitching fresh hay into the stalls when Sydney and Tucker returned. While Tucker unsaddled their mounts, she'd made a quick call to Esther. The package containing the USB thumb drive was yet to arrive, but most of the family was already there.

The wrangler had offered to take care of Beauty and the sorrel so they could meet the others at the house.

"I'm not going to dinner looking like this," Sydney said, as they walked back to the house.

"You look damned cute to me and there's definitely no dress code on the Double K."

"I smell like horseflesh."

"You'll fit right in."

"I'm sure my hair is going in a hundred different directions."

"More like fifty." Tucker reached down and tucked loose locks behind her ear.

"I promise I'll make it a quick shower and

change. Your family is probably already tired of waiting on us."

"We're not late, but you'd best go in by way of your patio or you'll get ambushed on your way there and never get to the shower."

"Good idea."

"Do you need me to go through the house and unlock it for you or did you leave it open?"

"It's locked, but the key's in my pocket."

He walked her to the door and lingered just long enough to make the moment awkward. The kiss was between them now and that changed everything no matter what they told each other.

Another time, another place and things might have been different, but all her focus had to be on rescuing Rachel. A mistake in judgment could be fatal. That bit of wisdom was forever seared into her mind.

She stripped from her clothes, dropping them on the vanity before stepping into the shower. As she lathered the shampoo into her short hair, unbidden memories rushed into her mind. The body of the beautiful college coed, naked, facedown in the murky bayou, waiting to be the next meal of a hungry alligator.

The Strangler's hands around Sydney's

neck, a second away from death. A lifetime of experiences hadn't raced through her mind as people often said. The past hadn't given her the strength to keep fighting. It was the dreams of the future that had made her keep fighting.

Those dreams were forever lost to Sara Goodwin. Sydney couldn't let them be lost for Rachel and the other captives.

She finished her shower and pulled a blue sundress from the small guest room closet. Casual, not too revealing, not too slouchy.

Now, if she could just ready her mind for family time. A very *brief* family time before she went back to the work of analyzing what they had so far, hopefully with new data from Dani's security film.

One solid clue. That might be all it took, but she needed it now.

SYDNEY HAD ZERO appetite when she joined the women and girls in the busy kitchen. The smell of frying chicken quickly took care of that.

"You made it," Esther said. "I was worried that horse-riding adventure might have left you plumb tuckered out what with you being up since dawn."

"I'm fine, just needed a quick shower."

"I love that dress," Dani said.

"Thank you. It's the only dress I brought with me. Everything else is business skirts and slacks and two pair of jeans. I wasn't expecting to do any socializing."

"I'm glad we thought of your moving in here," Dani said. "You need real meals. Mental work needs as much fuel as physical tasks. Plus you got a little physical exertion in today, too."

"It's all part of the process," Sydney said. "I go wherever the investigation takes me."

"Just stay safe," Esther cautioned. "Let your gun do your talking."

"Grandma," Constance said. "You want her to shoot people?"

"If they need it."

"Perhaps we should change the subject," Dani said. "Anyone have good news?"

"Well, I was planning to wear a sundress myself tonight," Grace said. "It's one I bought just two months ago, but when I put it on, it was a little too snug." She smiled conspiratorially, pulled her loose blouse tight and patted a small bulge in her stomach.

"Lord a mercy!" Esther squealed. "You're pregnant! I knew it when you turned that ugly shade of green and rushed from the breakfast table last week."

"You were right. But it's official now. Saw the doctor again and I'm in my second trimester."

The room erupted into hugs and congratulations.

Jaci started dancing around the room and singing at the top of her very healthy lungs. "I already knew it. I already knew it. I'm going to be a big sister. I already knew."

"You are so lucky," Constance said.

"I guess that means Pierce knows, too," Dani said.

"Yes. He's had as hard a time keeping it a secret this long as I have. He might be a teensy bit upset that I didn't wait until he was here to make the announcement. But I couldn't keep it in a second longer. It just bubbled right out of me."

"We're gonna have a baby around here," Esther said. "I just wish my Charlie was here to see it." She hummed a lullaby as she went back to transferring pieces of golden fried chicken from a deep fryer to an already-overflowing platter.

Sydney thought about the troubling statement Dudley had made that afternoon. If Dudley didn't tell the truth in court, Charlie would. He was not willing to see Dudley in prison for his spoiled and irresponsible daughter's crime.

It was the mark of a good friend. But had it cost Charlie his life? If so, knowing the facts wouldn't bring Charlie back. But would it ease Esther's mind or just bring all the pain and grief to the surface again?

Either way, if Charlie Kavanaugh had been murdered, he deserved justice. She'd look more into that later.

"Sydney, would you mind getting the butter from the fridge? I think these potatoes need a bit more."

"Sure. How much do you want? I'll cut it for you."

"Another fourth of a stick." Dani continued beating a huge bowl of potatoes with a hand mixer.

Grace stepped around Sydney and pulled a pan of fluffy biscuits from the oven. It defied logic that this many women could be cooking in one kitchen and making it seem more like a party than work.

Even the youngsters were busy. Constance sliced bananas with a table knife and Jaci layered a glass baking dish with vanilla wafers, all but the one she'd just slipped between her lips.

"How can I help?" Sydney asked.

"You just sit down and keep us company," Esther said. "You don't want to hurt the hand or get the bandage soiled."

"I'll change it anyway before I go to bed and the hand doesn't hurt unless I hit it against something or try to make a fist."

"You can oversee Jaci and Constance's project," Grace said. "The custard is in the saucepan on the front left burner, slightly cooled and ready to pour as soon as the girls have their first layer in place."

"I think I can handle that."

Sydney felt at home almost immediately. She'd come from a small family, just her, Rachel and their dad. This was her first experience being even a temporary part of a family this big, boisterous and caring.

Even more amazing, they weren't your typical family. Esther was clearly loved by everyone but actually kin to none. Jaci was Grace's stepdaughter. Constance was Dani's niece.

All held together by love, laughter and no doubt a few tears. She wondered how she'd fit into a family like this when so much of her time was spent dealing with the uglier side of life.

Definitely not something she needed to be concerned about tonight. One banana did not make a pudding. One horseback ride did not make her a cowgirl. One kiss did not equate with forever.

AN HOUR AND a half later, dinner was reduced to a few leftovers, the kitchen was clean with much help from the men and the film had still not arrived.

Stuffed and ready to relax, the whole family settled in the family den.

Uncle Tucker was clearly the star of the evening. Jaci climbed into his lap. Constance snuggled next to him on the wide leather sofa.

"Uncle Tucker, can you please stay until Saturday afternoon so you can watch me barrel race in our weekly rodeo? Please." Constance put her hands together in prayer form as she pleaded.

"I'll do my best," Tucker said. "Riley told me how good you are."

"She's already accumulated more points than some of the seventh graders," Riley said.

"And I've only lost my hat a couple of times all summer."

"Style is very important in barrel racing," Tucker said.

"I know. One time the wind blew it off, so you can't really count that."

"Absolutely not."

"And you can watch me do the mutton busting," Jaci said. "You can watch me, too, Sydney. I think I might win."

"I hope you win," Sydney said. "What is mutton busting?"

Jaci's eyes grew wide and she slapped her hand over her mouth to demonstrate her total shock. "You are a full-grown woman and you've never heard of mutton busting?"

"No. It's a good thing I have you to explain it to me."

"Well, you better come and watch so you'll know everything about it. First they put a helmet on my head, and then they sit me on the back of a sheep. When they let go, the sheep starts running as fast as it can. I just hang on until I tumble off."

"Does that hurt?"

"No. Sheep are little. They just like to run fast. It's fun, especially if you win."

"Right on," Tucker said. "Hanging on is the most important part."

"Speaking of holding on, let's check out the PBR network and see what the bull riders are doing," Riley said. He picked up the remote, turned on the TV and switched to the bull-riding channel.

The volume was too low to hear what the announcer on screen was saying, but the caption running below the picture said it all.

Rodeos have moment of silence in memory of Rod Hernandez.

Esther planted her feet and stopped the movement of her rocking chair. "Oh, no. Did you hear that, Tucker? Rod Hernandez. Dead. Wasn't he a friend of yours?"

"We were close."

"Did you know about this?"

"I did."

"Was he killed by the bull?" Esther asked. Her fears for Tucker shook her voice.

Riley turned off the TV. "Maybe we should table this conversation until later."

"I really need to be going," Grace said. "Jaci has school tomorrow."

"Same here," Dani added.

Tucker said nothing. This was clearly why he'd seemed so distant at times. He'd been grieving the death of his friend and hadn't wanted to upset her with his problems. Nor had he wanted to give Esther reason to worry about him.

The doorbell rang while they were gathering their things.

"I'll get it," Tucker volunteered. Sydney followed him to the door.

The visitor had a star pinned to the breast of his khaki uniform.

The security film had arrived.

Chapter Fourteen

Tucker handled the quick introductions between Sydney and the sheriff and then left them alone.

The sheriff peeked inside the open door. “Sounds like a party going on inside.”

“Esther hosted a family dinner in honor of Tucker’s visit.”

“I don’t want to interrupt your meal.”

“You’re not. We’ve finished and most are in the process of leaving.”

“Good. I need to talk to you about something in private.”

“I have a room of my own. We can talk there.”

“If it’s all the same with you, can we just take a short walk lest the mosquitoes get too bad to stay outside? I’ve been sitting at my desk for the last two hours finishing up some dadburn paperwork the county requires. Too much sittin' and my arthritis starts acting out."

"A walk would be fine."

Once they were down the steps, he took a worn path that trailed around the side of the house. "Jackson Clark speaks mighty highly of you," Cavazos said.

"I'm glad to hear that. I have great respect for him."

"He seems like a good man. Reasonable about most things. Here's the problem I'm having with all this. You FBI people come in here with lots of good ideas and every resource imaginable."

"It can be very effective," Sydney answered. Wherever this was going, she doubted she was going to like it.

"You got the know-how, but I know my folks. I know who to push for information, who to back away from. When and where to tread lightly."

Now she knew exactly where he was going. "Is this about Tucker and my visit to Dudley Miles this afternoon?"

"You might say that. It's about his wife, Millie. She's a good woman but she's had a hard go of it these last two years. Family problems that just tore her apart."

"I realize that," Sydney assured him. "What's your point?"

"Dudley says she got awfully upset when you were there today. She's scared you're trying to drag up the past and she just can't take no more trouble."

"We didn't even see her. She was supposedly in her room napping. How did she know we were there?"

"I reckon she caught a glimpse of you from her window when you were coming or going."

"I can understand how she knew Tucker. He's an old family friend. She's never met me. How could she know I'm an FBI agent?"

"She's seen you in town. Everyone has. You've been in most every store at least once and were even out at Hank's a couple of times. Winding Creek's a mind-everybody's-business kind of town."

"And yet no one seems to know anything about the four women who disappeared from this area."

"Yep. That's a strange one, which leads me to think that the perp is not from around here. My hunch is that it's someone who makes deliveries or travels through here for some other reason on a regular basis."

"We can't rule out that he is from around here. For one thing, how would he happen to pick all nonlocals for his victims if he didn't know the area?"

"You've got me there. All I'm saying for sure is if you need to see Dudley again, I'd appreciate it if you'd go through me. I can ask the questions for you or he said he'd meet you at my office anytime. He just don't want to get Millie all riled up."

"He offered me twenty-five thousand dollars in reward money."

"He's bringing the check by my office in the morning. I'll leave it to you and Jackson to decide how to get the word out."

"Fair enough. Have you seen any of the security film yet?"

"Not yet, but one of my deputies looked over the portion of the tape I brought you. It covers a two-hour time slot that includes the time period before Rachel entered Dani's Delights until well after she leaves. He didn't spot anything out of the ordinary, though he did mention it would be nice to be able to hear instead of just see what was going on. Still, he figured the film was as useless as a knot in a stake rope."

Whatever that meant, she prayed it proved not to be true.

"One of my night clerks is copying all the tapes we confiscated today. That way I can get them to Jackson first thing in the morning."

"That will be a big help."

"Something better help soon. Whole county's chewing their bit—men scared to let their wives and daughters out of the house by themselves. That's why I wanted to be sure and get this to you tonight."

Nor did he want to miss warning her not to upset Millie Miles.

"Guess that about does it for now," Cavazos said. "I'll let you get inside and get some rest."

"I'll be burning the midnight oil tonight," she said, "starting with the security tape."

"If you're half as good as Jackson claims, you might have this all figured out by morning."

"I know Jackson didn't promise you that."

"'Bout damn near it." He handed her the small brown envelope that held the thumb drive. "A change of subject, but do you reckon Esther's got some of that dinner left?"

"I'm sure she does."

They'd reached the back of the sprawling house. From this point the path they'd taken meandered past a nearby woodshed. Sydney's small patio was a few yards to the right.

"When you see her, tell her that you walked me to my patio door and I went in to get some work done."

"Will do. And thanks for understanding about Millie."

She understood, but that didn't mean she'd grant his request. Lives were on the line.

SYDNEY KICKED OFF her white sandals and switched on her laptop. Anxiety rode her nerves again. Four women's lives might be riding on what she did or didn't discover.

If the deputy didn't see anything that looked suspicious, then Rachel must have been alone. Best scenario now was to spot someone or something that raised questions in her mind.

She took her computer, small notebook and a pen to an upholstered chair tucked away in the corner of the room. She missed her office with its large desk and work area and a huge wall for charting her findings.

She was fifteen minutes into the digital recording when she got her first glimpse of Rachel entering the shop. Her breath caught. Her sweet sister, relaxed, stunning in a flowing, summery dress.

She was immediately struck by the desire to stop the frame and let that image soak in, but her mind overrode her emotions. She needed to see everything that transpired exactly as she would have seen it if she'd been there the first time.

She would replay it many times before the night was over.

Rachel was alone. She stopped momentarily before getting in a line that stretched almost to the door. Two teenage girls were in front of her, both on their cell phones. An elderly couple with two preteen boys—likely their grandsons—were behind her.

No doubt bored from the inactivity, the boys started some horseplay. One shoved playfully; the other fell into Rachel. She laughed it off, though it was evident the gentleman was scolding the boys. After that, Rachel and the grandmother got into what was obviously a friendly conversation.

That was the extent of Rachel's involvement with strangers until she reached the counter.

Dani greeted her with a smile and then bagged Rachel's pastry while the same cute teenage girl who'd been helping out today served as barista.

Instead of taking a seat, Rachel perused the gift items while she sipped her coffee, the pastry still in its bag. At one point, she picked up a colorful coffee mug, checked the price and returned it to the shelf.

She didn't speak to anyone until she reached the pottery display. Two men who appeared to be in their midtwenties seemed to be comparing two tall vases.

A minute later they engaged in an animated conversation with Rachel. No sign of confrontation or disagreement. Eventually, Rachel decided on a bowl and went back to the counter to pay for it.

She talked with Dani as she completed the credit-card transaction and carefully bound the bowl in protective wrap. Rachel returned the wallet to her handbag, took her package and left, balancing her bowl, pastry and coffee.

A man who was coming in as she was leaving held the door for her.

That was it.

Rachel hadn't pulled out a roll of cash at the register, hadn't engaged with any men except the two extremely unlikely suspects at the pottery display, and her only run-in had been with a mischievous kid who accidentally bumped into her.

Worthless as a knot in a stake. She had to ask Tucker what that meant.

She was glad Tucker was giving her this time alone to work but she wondered if she'd see him again tonight. If he did come in to say good-night, then what?

The kiss was still on her mind, just tangled with the ever-increasing urgency of finding Rachel. The intensity of her attraction toward him had accelerated so fast she was afraid to trust her emotions.

One thing was for certain: she'd never let any other man into her life so quickly. Had never once been blown away by a kiss.

She rewound the tape and started it over at the point just before Rachel entered the store.

She paused the play immediately. She'd been so intent on Rachel's movements that she hadn't noticed the woman who'd been leaving the bakery as Rachel entered.

Even now she couldn't be certain, as much

of the woman's face was blocked by the door, but it looked like Millie Miles. Sydney quickly zoomed in on the image.

She was almost sure it was Millie. Not that her being at the bakery at the same time as Rachel carried any suspicious connotations, but the Miles family were popping into this investigation on a regular basis.

Other than Millie catching Sydney's attention, the second viewing gave her nothing. Neither did the third.

Disappointment had reached new levels, but she was nowhere near ready to give it up for the night. She'd brush her teeth, wash her face and change her bandage before she started charting everything she knew about every element of this investigation.

Few serial perps had ever chosen their victims strictly at random. Something triggered their acts.

Unless the perp was completely mad.

TUCKER HESITATED AT the closed door to Sydney's room. He didn't want to make her think he was being pushy by interrupting her while she was working. Yet he couldn't just ignore the fact that she might need his company after viewing the film.

He tapped softly.

"Who is it?"

"Tucker."

"Come in if you dare."

Neither the words nor the tone were welcoming. He opened the door and peeked inside. The floor was littered with markers, tiny stick-on stars, tape and white poster board. Presumably, the supplies she'd picked up in town earlier today.

"An art project?"

"If it is, I'm failing badly. Take a seat if you can find one."

He dropped to the edge of the bed. Sydney was sitting cross-legged on the floor, sticking stars on a detailed map of Winding Creek and the surrounding area that had been taped to a large square of poster board.

"How did your talk with Esther go?" Sydney asked.

"She thinks I'm a hardheaded, macho imbecile who thinks it's cool to try and get myself killed just for the fun of it. Other than that, she loves me."

"You can't blame her for worrying."

"I don't blame her. I'm not even sure she's wrong. That's an interesting map," Tucker said, ready to change the subject. "Where did you get it?"

"It was in the folder Jackson passed out at the first meeting along with the personal data of the women who'd been reported missing. All except for Rachel's. I had to fill everyone in on her."

"What do the stars represent?"

"The blue stars show the last place the women were known to be before they disappeared."

"What do the numbered stars next to the blue stars represent?"

"The order in which they went missing. The time of day they were last seen is printed on the white strip stickers."

Tucker stooped on his haunches to get a better look.

"I'm looking for a pattern," Sydney explained. "The pictured representations tend to make them pop out at you better than a table of printed facts."

"Just like on the cop shows on TV."

"Yes, except I tend to go overboard with all the facts I like to include. I'm a visual learner."

"Makes it easy to see how fast the frequency of the abduction is escalating," Tucker said. "One six months ago. One three months ago. And now two in the past six weeks."

"And then he's likely responsible for Sara Goodwin's death and no one knows for sure yet when she went missing."

"Guy is definitely brazen."

"Or he has mental problems that are worsening," Sydney said. "Here's what we know so far. The missing women are all attractive brunettes who were traveling alone. Since they were all last seen in this area, I assume he hooked up with them at some spot in or around Winding Creek."

"Except for Rachel's car, none of the women's vehicles have been found," Tucker added. "It could be that he has a place to dump them where they haven't been found and he ran out of space."

"Good point. But he has to make sure no one sees him driving their car."

"Maybe he forces them to drive him somewhere, and then he k..." Tucker stopped short. Sydney knew as well as he did that there was a chance all the missing women were dead, but she'd avoided saying it out loud.

He got that. Positive thoughts were far more productive.

"I think the perp either lives in Winding Creek or near here," Sydney said. "He's somewhat of a loner. For some reason, he spends a lot of time in town. When forced to interact, he holds it together so that people may think he's odd, but don't realize how mentally unbalanced he is.

"He may not be actively looking for victims, but something he sees in a woman triggers the violent nature he may have kept in check for years until something happened to change that."

"You are good at this," Tucker said.

"I could be way off track," she admitted, "but I don't think so. What I can't figure out is how he gets the women to go with him. Is it willingly? Or does he overpower them? If so, how does he do that over and over without being seen? And where are they now? Prisoners in his house or some isolated location where no one goes except him?"

"Most every ranch except the very smallest has old, dilapidated structures somewhere on their land. Barns that haven't been used in years. Rotting sheds filled with nothing but spiders, snakes and rusting tools. The problem is it would take weeks or maybe months to search them all."

"That's why we have to keep narrowing this down."

"And cover this town and surrounding areas with posters offering that reward Dudley promised," Tucker said. "That would get everyone looking for this guy on their own land, doing your work for you."

"Or getting themselves killed trying to apprehend him. We have to stress that all we want is information. No one is to go after this man on his own."

"Lot of luck with getting that message across," Tucker said. "This is rural Texas. I'd wager most cowboys or ranchers carry a gun in their vehicle or have one with them when they're out working. For protection from snakes, not people. But they know how to shoot."

"Still, we have to stress the perp is dangerous. I'll work on designing the poster tonight."

"Did you get anything enlightening from Dani's security film?"

"No. It seemed like business as usual. Rachel was alone. She talked to several people, but nothing that looked the least bit threatening. She did talk to two men about pottery. I'll ask Dani about them, but I didn't get any bad vibes."

"Rotten news."

"Yeah. That's why I'm back to the drawing board. Millie Miles made an appearance, but she was leaving as Rachel was arriving. I don't know if the sheriff mentioned it to you, but he said my visit upset Millie and that Dudley doesn't want me on the ranch again."

"He mentioned it. I told him to stuff it—in a gentlemanly way, of course."

"Of course."

Sydney picked up the markers and loose stars and dropped them into plastic bags.

"Through working for tonight?"

"Through with the art part, not nearly through with the thinking and searching for any pattern that could lead us to the freak."

Tucker helped her pick up the rest of her supplies. When he finished, he went back to his perch on the edge of the bed. To his surprise, she walked over and sat down beside him.

Their thighs touched. Inconspicuously. Unintentionally, he was sure. His chest tightened and his manly urges checked in as if on autopilot. She put her hand on his arm, and when he met her gaze, he felt the heat deep inside him.

"Is something wrong?" she asked. "Why are you looking at me that way?"

"I don't think you really want me to answer that question."

"I wouldn't have asked if I didn't want to know."

"I'm thinking how gorgeous you look tonight. I love you in jeans. But you look delectable in that dress. To be honest, it's all I can do not to take you in my arms right now."

Her lips on his was her unexpected response. Passion exploded like fireworks. He kissed her lips, the tip of her nose, her eyelids and then back to her lips again. He couldn't get enough of her. Every part of his body craved more.

Yet when she pulled away, he forced himself to let her go.

"I know I started this but I can't keep doing this, Tucker. It's not you. You do everything right. It's just that my emotions are so raw and unprotected right now."

"You don't have to say more. I'll never push

you into anything you're not ready for. When the time is right, we'll both know."

"Thanks. I'm going to the bathroom to get ready for bed," she said, "but only because I'll fall asleep working. You should probably be gone when I come back."

His mouth didn't argue the point. His body did. It was hell watching her walk away.

SYDNEY CLOSED THE bathroom door and leaned against it, struggling to put everything in some kind of perspective that made sense. Her concern for Rachel was ripping her heart from her chest.

How could she feel this level of attraction for a man she'd just met?

The only explanation was that the heart-wrenching feeling of helplessness was making her emotionally vulnerable. Tucker wasn't just an incredibly virile hunk. He was smart, thoughtful, protective.

It would be only natural that he'd stir strong feelings inside her. When this was over, when Rachel and the others were safe and the world tilted back on its axis, she'd figure this out.

Until then, she couldn't let anyone affect her focus—not even Tucker Lawrence.

She pulled a pair of pink flowered shorty pajamas from the drawer beneath the dressing table. Simple, comfortable and unsexy pajamas just in case Tucker came back.

She took her time washing and creaming her face while struggling to regain her proper focus, though her energy was beginning to falter.

It was at least five minutes later when she opened the door and stepped back into the bedroom.

Tucker had not left. He was stretched out on her bed on top of the covers, fully clothed except for his boots. His head rested on her pillow. His eyes were closed.

He was snoring, not the house-shaking racket her dad used to make, but nonetheless loud enough there was no doubt that he was sound asleep.

Temptation took an unbidden turn, and she experienced an almost-overwhelming desire to crawl into bed beside him. Not to make love, just to feel her body lying next to his for a few brief moments.

Instead she went back to her computer and spent the next few hours going over every tidbit of information she had yet again.

Eventually, the words began to blur and her thoughts got lost in a fog. She glanced at the clock. It was 2:00 a.m. Tucker was still asleep. She suspected he hadn't been sleeping well after watching his good friend die so tragically. Either that or *not* making love had worn him out.

Her mind was muddled from exhaustion. She didn't have the energy or the inclination to wake him up. She stepped out of her slippers, flicked off the light and crawled into bed beside him. Caught somewhere between levels of consciousness, she cuddled against him.

He made her feel safe.

Chapter Fifteen

Thursday, September 21

Tucker woke to a sharp blow to his stomach and low growling and moaning sounds in his ear. He realized where he was and what was going on just in time to avoid another jab to his body, not from a fist but Sydney's elbow.

He pulled her into his arms and rocked her against him. "I've got you, baby. You're safe. It's all good, just a nightmare."

She jerked away from him and sat up in bed.

"Tucker?"

"It's me." He didn't remember falling asleep in this bed, but obviously he had.

"You're still here?"

"Looks that way. Not intentionally," he assured her. "I've been sound asleep. Bed is too damn comfortable." He'd only planned to stay in her room long enough to make sure she was okay after her abrupt escape to the bathroom.

That was the last thing he remembered.

She lay back down, her hands cradling her head as she stared at the ceiling. "It's fine. Again, not your fault. I could have sent you away at any time, but I just crawled into bed with you."

She rolled over to face him. "You're safe. I was too tired to jump your bones."

Moonlight and shadows played on her face, just enough light to see the fear that still gripped her, the fear she was trying to cover up with a light banter he wasn't buying.

"Must have been a tough nightmare," he said. "Want to talk about it?"

"It was bizarre," she said. "Things were twisted. The Swamp Strangler was chasing me through the swamp but Rachel was with him and I didn't know if she was trying to help me or kill me. There were dead bodies all around us. Only their eyes were open and they were looking at me."

The nightmare still held sway over her emotions. He could hear the torment in her voice.

He ached to hold her tight and comfort her, but that could be the worst move he could make. He basically understood nothing about women.

"I'm fighting the Swamp Strangler all over again," she murmured. "I think that's all in the past, and then he invades my thoughts and dreams. What if he's affecting my ability to do my job?"

He remembered hearing about the Swamp Strangler, a south Louisiana serial killer who raped his victims and then left their bodies in murky waters of a bayou to be eaten by the alligators. He didn't remember exactly how he was captured.

"Were you in on that case?" he asked.

"Yes. I profiled him, and then realized who his next victim would be and where he would be taking her. When I couldn't reach her by phone, I knew if someone didn't stop him immediately, it would be too late."

He could see where this was going and sense how upset she was getting just talking about it. "You don't have to go there now, Sydney. He's dead. He's done with."

"I was too late," she said. "Minutes too late. I saw the body facedown in the water and knew it was too late. I went after him, chasing him through bog so damp and spongy I was afraid I'd get sucked into it too deep to ever escape."

Her body trembled and he could stand it no longer. Tucker pulled her back into his arms. "It's over, baby."

"But it wasn't over. This was his world and he used his mastery of the environment to capture me. I felt his fingers tightening on my throat. I felt life ebbing away. And I knew I wasn't ready to die.

"Somehow I got to the tiny gun hidden inside my wristband and put six bullets into his body before he lost his grip on my throat."

He held her, not saying a word while the strain and tension slowly let go of her body. He knew the grief and mental upheaval of watching a close friend die. It might totally destroy Sydney to find that she'd failed in saving her sister's life.

Yet all he could think of was keeping Sydney safe.

"Don't take chances this time, Sydney. Promise me you won't go after this lunatic alone."

"I promise."

He wasn't convinced. She burrowed her head under his chin and scrunched against him.

Damn. The urges hit again, his whole body aching to make love with her.

"I need to go back to my room and let you get some sleep," he whispered.

"You can stay," she whispered.

The invitation was clear. He wanted to accept so badly that walking away would just about kill him. But sometimes a man just had to do what a man had to do.

"Not tonight, Sydney. I can't stay and not make love with you, and I don't want our first time to be tainted by anguish. I want it to be a night you remember forever because I know I will."

He kissed her lightly and then got up quickly. He had to get the hell out of here while he still could.

SYDNEY OPENED HER EYES. Sunshine flooded the bedroom. She rolled over quickly and checked her phone. Eight o'clock. She never slept this late when she was working. How had she let this happen? Exhaustion was no excuse.

She kicked off the sheet but made the mistake of glancing across the bed to the spot where she'd lain in Tucker's arms during the wee hours of the morning.

She let her hand slide to the pillow, still wrinkled from the weight of his head. His musky scent filled her senses.

At this moment she felt closer to him than she'd ever felt to any other man. She'd shared more of her fears, let him see deep inside the part of herself she normally kept secret, and she'd only known him since Monday.

Enough. She'd have to figure out any relationship that might or might not happen when her mind was clear and her emotions weren't in free fall. When the current madness was over and the relentless abductor was behind bars.

She dressed hurriedly, slipping into a pair of white capris and a pale blue pullover shirt. She didn't bother with makeup but calmed her mussed hair with a brush before heading toward the kitchen.

The house was unusually quiet, though odors of bacon, cinnamon and coffee hung heavy in the air. When she reached the kitchen, it was clear that breakfast was over and done with. The table had been cleared. The dishwasher was running.

She lifted the coffeepot. It was full. Evidently Esther had made a fresh pot before they'd all left to go about their lives. As it should be. Her life had been consuming theirs.

She poured a cup of coffee and was about to call and check in with Jackson when she heard the back door open. Esther was singing an old Frank Sinatra standard when she stepped into the kitchen with a basket of fresh hen's eggs over one arm and a basket of yellow squash over the other.

"Good morning," Esther said. "Sorry I wasn't here when you got up, but I have to get outside and do a little gathering and harvesting before it gets too hot. If we don't get a break in this heat soon, I may have to go on one of those Alaskan cruises my friends keep talking about."

"You should," Sydney said.

"Have you ever been there?"

"No, but I've always wanted to. Maybe next summer the two of us can go up there and explore the glaciers."

"I'd like that."

As strange as it was to admit it, Sydney

would like that, too. Three days and she was already feeling part of the family. There was probably a hidden meaning there that she wasn't going to get caught up in this morning.

"The guys finished up breakfast early today," Esther said. "Price of beef is up right now and they're helping Pierce check his livestock, deciding which ones to take to market this month and how many to feed and fatten awhile longer."

"Before this week, I had no idea how complicated or how time-consuming ranching is. Nor would I have guessed how dedicated these Texas cowboys are to their lifestyles."

"Cowgirls, too," Esther said. "Once it gets in your blood, there's no getting it out."

"What about your friend Millie Miles? Is she one of those rancher's wives who would hate living anywhere except on the ranch?"

Esther shook her head and started putting away the eggs. "That Millie is a horse of a different color. She's one of those heiresses, spoiled by all that fancy stuff from the day she was born. Her father died in his fifties and all the money from his software fortune fell into her bank account like manna from heaven."

"Really. She seems quite a bit younger than

Dudley. I assumed she'd married him for his money."

"Nope. Not that Dudley was poor, mind you. His daddy left him that huge stretch of land he lives on and one of the most prosperous cattle operations in this part of Texas. I reckon they fell in love either with each other or the idea of being in love. I was never sure which."

"Then you don't think they're happily married now?"

"I think she went off the deep end the day her grandson's body was found, and then fell to rock bottom when her daughter went to prison. Looks worse every time I see her, like a woman on her way to meet the devil who knows there's no turning back."

An odd analogy. Esther, with all her Texas roots, had a way of saying things that cut right through to the truth.

Sydney's cell phone rang. It was Jackson.

She excused herself and walked into the hall to take the call in private.

"Did you get a chance to look at the film that Cavazos dropped off?"

"I did. It led nowhere."

"Then let's move on. Lane just sent me a

digital composition that combines and frames photos from seven different security cameras around Winding Creek. We can analyze who was in what store at what time on what day and compare it with what we know about where the victims were last seen."

"God bless Lane and his willingness to give up sleep for work."

"You must be doing some of the same," Jackson said. "The file you sent with the design for the award poster was dated in the wee hours."

"When I was brain-dead," she said. "I hope it makes sense."

"Looked good to me. I've passed it on to the sheriff. His people will post it immediately on a Winding Creek website and also post paper copies of it all over town."

"That's a start. When do I get Lane's file?"

"That's why I'm calling. Head over this way now. The rest of the team is on the way. Let's brainstorm our way through this and figure it out. I have a strong hunch that our depraved perp is about to make his next move."

Jackson was known for the accuracy of his hunches.

Chapter Sixteen

Sydney pulled into the drive at Jackson's temporary office setup as Rene, Allan and Tim were climbing out of Rene's personal SUV. Tim carried a large white bag with the top folded over several times. Allan carried a box of doughnuts.

Tim waited until she caught up with them and held the door for her.

"I hope there's something healthy to eat in the bag," she said.

"*Delicioso* tacos," Tim said. "With jalapeños and extra hot sauce. You're gonna love them."

"And for your information, these doughnuts are super nutritious," Allan informed her. "Grease, flour, sugar. All the main food groups."

"Not to worry," Rene said. "The boss specifically ordered a non-spicy breakfast taco for you. He has high hopes for you breaking the secret code to help find the Lone Star Snatcher."

Sydney hurried to catch up with Rene. "What did you call him?"

"Damn it. Sorry, Sydney. I didn't mean to let that slip in front of you."

"Let that slip? Does that mean you guys have been referring to the perp that way all week and keeping it from me?"

"It just slipped out of my mouth one day when we were talking," Tim said. "You know it's not that we're not taking this case dead serious. It's just force of habit to give worthless scum like our perp a nickname."

"Never meant to offend you," Rene added as they walked back toward the kitchen.

Another of the problems with her being personally involved in the case. They were worried about her sensitivities when they needed to all be talking freely.

"I'm not offended," she assured them. "I know how serious you all are about apprehending the perp and saving Rachel and the others. Rest assured, that is nowhere near as repulsive as what I've been calling him in my mind."

"You're seriously okay with it?" Allan asked.

"Seriously. I don't care what you call him. Let's just bring him down."

They were all in favor of that.

Eager to get started, they passed out the food and poured the coffee in no time flat. After a few more minutes to adjust the equipment delivered from Jackson's Dallas office that morning, the spliced and edited version of the film was showing on a large portable screen.

"If you see anything you want to comment on, let me know and I'll pause the frame," Tim said.

The film started on March 9 at 2:45 p.m. and had been taken from the Chic Cowgirl Boutique, where Alice Baker from Shreveport, Louisiana, charged a pair of expensive boots at 3:30 p.m.

"She looks relaxed," Tim commented.

"Definitely alone."

"Pause," Allan said. "Not a clear image, but check out the tall cowboy with the sexy young blonde. I'm almost sure I saw him in the drugstore last night with a different blonde, also very attractive. He was picking up a prescription while I was buying shaving cream."

"Probably just a playboy but keep an eye out for him moving forward," Jackson said.

"Notice the older guy looking at the boots on the sale rack," Tim said. "He keeps turning around to look at Alice while she's admiring her boots in the mirror."

From the boot shop the film composite progressed to other Winding Creek locations, same day, both before and after her trip to the boutique. Alice wasn't seen again.

Shopping for boots might have been her fatal mistake.

This continued for what seemed like forever until they finally hit a speck of pay dirt. The last record for Michelle Dickens was a charge at an Exxon station just out of San Antonio. Nothing had placed her in or within forty miles of Winding Creek.

But there she was, perusing the local candle shop on August 20, the day she disappeared.

The shop was almost empty and the only person in there who looked even vaguely familiar to Sydney was the woman in charge of the shop.

And Millie Miles. For a woman who didn't

even have the energy to drive anymore, she sure made it into town often enough.

"Whoa. Hold it right there," Sydney said. "The woman in the white pantsuit is Millie Miles. It probably means nothing but I also saw her leaving Dani's Delights just as Rachel was walking in."

"We may see several people more than once," Jackson said, "but still worth noting. It definitely appears that all roads lead to and leave from Winding Creek."

They finished the morning with the tape at Dani's Delights that Sydney had looked at over and over last night. She wasn't up to seeing it again.

She slipped out of the kitchen and onto the back porch. The day was already sweltering. Her spirits were scraping bottom. She checked her phone for missed messages and found one from Tucker.

She called him back immediately. His voice didn't cheer her, but all the same it felt good to hear him say hello.

"Sorry I missed you this morning," he said. "Pierce wanted some other opinions and I didn't want to wake you."

"That's fine. Jackson wouldn't have approved your attending this meeting anyway."

"You sound down," he said. "I hope it's not from bad news."

"No. It's from having no news. Nothing to jump-start the search or even nudge it forward."

"Hate to hear that. I'm back at Esther's. Do you want to meet for lunch? All I have to do is grab a quick shower."

"I'll need to call you back and let you know. This is Jackson's meeting and I'm not sure what he has in mind next."

"No worries. Just give me a call. I'm easy."

"The faces are all starting to run together," Rene was saying as she rejoined them in the kitchen. "It's nearly one. I say we break for lunch."

"Just one quick follow-up question before we scatter," Tim said. "You may be the one to answer this one, Sydney. Are the Houston detectives still questioning your sister's ex-boyfriend?"

"He's been cleared," Jackson said. "Airtight alibi. Water-skiing up at Lake Conroe with friends from work all afternoon that Saturday."

"I never really considered him a suspect," Sydney said, "but glad they checked him out."

"I'll bet ninety to nothing the Snatcher drives a pickup truck," Tim said. "I've never seen so many in one small town. I'm starting to feel like a wimp in my sedan."

"And most of them black," Rene said.

"Agreed," Tim added. "With numerous scratches to the paint and a few layers of red Texas clay splattered around the tires to prove they don't belong to sissy city dwellers."

Sydney excused herself and went to the bathroom for relief and to freshen up. When she returned to the kitchen, Jackson was the only one in sight and he was on the phone.

"Whatever you do, don't let her out of your sight. I'll be right there.

"Grab your handbag, Sydney. The perp has struck again. Only this time the victim got away."

SHERIFF CAVAZOS MET them at the door to the County Sheriff's Office. "She's not hurt physically but she's an emotional wreck. She gave us a little information but then clammed up. Says she only wants to talk to a woman. I figure you're the best one for the job, Sydney."

"What's her name?"

"Joy White. She fits the same pattern as the other victims. Attractive. Brunette. Thirty-one years old. She's not from Winding Creek."

"Where is she from?" Sydney asked.

"I don't know. She teared up and started crying before we could find out where she was from or why she was here in Winding Creek today."

"Where was she when she was attacked?" Jackson asked.

"About ten miles out of town on the blacktop, what we natives refer to as the scenic drive back to the main highway. I've got a crime-scene team out there now, but feel free to send your guys out there, too, if it would make you feel better. I can give them directions."

"Thanks. I'll get hold of Allan and Rene and have them call you. I'll wait here to see what Sydney learns."

"Lead the way," Sydney said.

"Joy's in my office. I figured it would be less frightening for her than the cold, sterile interrogation areas."

"Good thinking."

The sheriff left Sydney at his office door.

She tapped softly. When no one answered, she opened the door and slipped inside.

She kept her voice low and calming. "My name is Sydney Maxwell, Joy. I'm with the FBI. I heard you had a close call this morning."

"He tried to kill me. I didn't do anything. He didn't know me. He just wanted to kill me." The words were broken, fighting their way out between short gasps of breath.

"I believe you and I know how scary that must have been."

"Why? Why me?"

"We think he may be the man responsible for the women who've gone missing from the Winding Creek area over the last few months. We need to stop him before he hurts someone else."

"He's crazy. I could see it in his eyes." She closed her eyes tight for a few moments before opening them again.

"Can you tell me what happened?" Sydney asked.

"How do I know he won't come after me again if I do? Are you going to protect me?"

"If you need protection, I'll see that you get

it. I know how afraid you are, Joy, but you got away. You're one of the lucky ones."

Joy covered her face with her hands. Sydney pulled up a chair so that they were facing each other, so close that their knees brushed when Joy shifted in her chair.

"My sister is one of the missing women, Joy. I don't know if she's dead or alive. I only know that she and at least three other women might still be his captives."

Dead or alive. The words were difficult to utter, but the truth refused to be silenced this time.

Joy uncovered her face and clasped her hands tightly in her lap. "Heaven help them." She wiped a tear from her cheek with the back of her hand. "What is it you want to know?"

"Everything, just the way it happened. Take your time. Don't leave anything out. I'll be right here with you. There are law-enforcement personnel all around. He can't hurt you now."

Finally, Joy opened up and the words tumbled from her lips, mostly coherent, sometimes stifled by a shudder.

Joy was a romance writer from Gruene, Texas, who'd driven to Winding Creek that morning to speak to a county-wide book-club meeting.

The library had a parking lot but it was full when Joy got there and she had to park two blocks away near the pharmacy on Main Street.

The only place she went after the meeting was to Dani's Delights to get an iced latte to drink on her way home. She hadn't seen her accoster at the library or in the bakery and hadn't realized he was following her until he drove up even with her on a two-lane road.

"He started waving his arms and yelling hysterically for me to pull over to the shoulder and stop the car. I tried to wave him off, but he looked so upset, I rolled down my window. He pointed to the back of my car and told me I was leaking gas and sparks were flying.

"I didn't see any smoke and I was afraid to stop. There were no other cars in sight and there were wooded areas on both sides of the blacktop."

"What made you stop?"

"He slowed and dropped behind me, still waving for me to pull over. Then I heard an explosion that sounded like it came from my trunk. I thought the car might be about to blow up."

"I can see why you would."

"I threw on my brakes as I pulled to the shoulder and jumped out of the car. There were no flames, no smoke, only this wild cowboy running toward me."

"What did you do then?"

"I panicked, jumped back in the car and grabbed my revolver from beneath the seat. Before I could lock the door, he yanked it open and was coming at me, both hands fisted.

"I shot and the bullet hit him in the right leg. Blood spurted everywhere. I didn't care. I kicked him away from my car and left him bleeding in the middle of the road. I drove all the way to the highway before I felt safe enough to pull over and call 911."

Tears started to flow down Joy's cheeks. "It's not my gun. My husband made me bring it because of all the trouble we've been hearing about. I've never shot a man before."

"You did the right thing, Joy. The brave thing. You may have saved the lives of many other women."

Now all Sydney needed from Joy was an

extremely accurate description, but the urgency had soared to its highest level yet.

The Lone Star Snatcher would be running scared and a psycho running scared was dangerously unpredictable.

ROY SALES PUT the whiskey bottle to his lips and gulped it down as if it were water. His leg hurt something fierce and whiskey was the only painkiller he had.

He was in big trouble now. The whole town would be talking about the attack. The sheriff, the FBI, even the Texas Rangers would be out to get him now.

They'd be looking for a man with a bullet wound in his right leg. They'd have his DNA and his description.

He couldn't even show his face at the big house to force Millie to give him more money. His sweet little blackmail deal was over. He'd done what she asked, killed on demand. Blew poor old Charlie Kavanaugh's brains out with him begging for mercy.

He didn't like to kill. He hadn't wanted to kill Charlie. He hadn't wanted to kill sweet little Sara Goodwin, but she'd called him a monster. A monster, after he'd picked her up off the street and taken her in.

She'd said he was crazy. He wasn't crazy. He did what he was told. Mommy didn't like it when he disobeyed. She didn't like to have to lock him in the cold, dark basement. She just wanted him to learn to be a good boy.

Mommy was yelling in his brain now. He put his hands over his ears and tried to shut her out, but she wouldn't stop. She never stopped. Even after he'd pushed her off the ladder and killed her, she wouldn't stop tormenting him.

Kill your prisoners. Kill your prisoners. Kill your prisoners and run for your life. Run, Roy. Run and never stop.

They weren't prisoners. They were his guests. He didn't want to kill them. He didn't like being alone at night when the voices came at him from all directions.

But he couldn't just leave the women here to tell all kinds of lies about him.

He'd burn the shack to the ground. That was it. There would be nothing but ashes. They might even think he'd burned with his guests and then they'd never come after him.

All except Rachel. He couldn't kill Rachel. She was starting to understand him. They were friends. His mother hated her, but that was too bad. This time he wouldn't listen to her no matter how loudly she screamed into his mind.

Rachel would be going with him.

It was time to start the fire.

Chapter Seventeen

They had their description. They knew how the kidnapper operated. Rene had even found a huge firecracker casing at the crime scene to explain the explosion.

It was progress. It just wasn't enough progress.

Sydney called Tucker as she left the sheriff's office and asked him to meet her at Dani's Delights so that she could explain the latest developments. The way he'd stood by her this week, he deserved to be kept in the loop.

And she wanted to see him. No use in hiding from the truth any longer. It didn't change anything at this point, but she was tired of fighting the unalterable fact. She was falling hard for the bull rider.

She drove the few blocks to Main Street and pulled into the angled parking spot between two black pickup trucks that had both edged over the white line and into her space.

Wide, long-bed, black pickup trucks. Her FBI team was right. The town was overrun with them. What did the cowboys have against magenta or deep burgundy?

Millie Miles stepped out of the passenger-side door of the truck to Sydney's right just as Sydney was stepping out of her car. This was obviously one of those days she hadn't wanted to drive. Why should she when she could just have one of her many wranglers to serve as chauffeur.

Or maybe she had the same chauffeur every day. Driving Mrs. Millie.

In town—on a regular basis like the day Rachel had been walking into Dani's Delights when Millie was walking out. Had Millie been in Winding Creek but perhaps in different shops whenever all of the victims had last been seen in Winding Creek?

It was a long shot but the best thing she had going now.

Sydney walked over to the truck, stopped

beside the driver's open window and introduced herself.

"Hi, I'm Sydney Maxwell with the FBI." She flashed her badge. "May I ask you a few questions?"

"Am I in trouble?"

"Not unless you've broken the law."

"I had a speeding ticket last year."

"I'll let you pass on that. I just noticed Millie Miles getting out of your truck. That's so nice of you to drive her around. Do you do that every day?"

"No. That's usually Roy Sales's job."

"Where is Roy today?"

"He was here earlier. He dropped the boss lady off at the library for some kind of meeting. He was supposed to come back and pick up her and a friend at Caffe's after lunch. He never showed. The friend got a ride home and I drew the flunky card. Don't tell the boss lady I put it that way."

"Never. What do you think happened to Roy Sales?"

"Who knows. He's like a blister. Annoying as hell and doesn't show up until the work is done, if you get my drift."

"I do. I think I may have met Roy before.

Does he have greasy brown hair that crawls into his shirt collar? A slight build. Short—only a few inches taller than me." As per Joy White's description except for leaving out the crazy look in his eyes.

"Yep. You've met him. That's him to a T."

Her heart burst into overdrive. This was the way it felt when all the pieces fell into place.

She thanked the driver for his trouble, rushed back to her car and put in a call to Jackson. She got his answering machine, which meant he was likely talking to someone else. He didn't like to be out of touch with his agents.

She left a message.

"I think we've got our man. Name's Roy Sales. Works for Dudley and Millie Miles. I'm headed out to Kurlacky Acres Ranch, where he lives now. Meet me there. Call Tucker for directions. And hurry."

Excitement and adrenaline rushed through her, but even that couldn't bury the surging fear. She had no idea what she'd find when she got to Roy's place.

She prayed as she pushed the accelerator nearly to the floor.

Please let Rachel be alive and well.

Let all the Snatcher's prisoners, however many there are, be safe.

SYDNEY ALMOST PASSED the rickety gate before she saw it. She slammed on her brakes and swerved into the dirt and grass of the drive.

It occurred to her that she didn't know where to go once she was through the gate. Tucker had said there were shacks, sheds and dilapidated barns scattered all over some of the ranches.

The smart thing to do would be to pull her small rental car into one of the wooded areas she could see from here and wait for Jackson. She couldn't afford any stupid mistakes this time.

With luck, Roy would be working at Dudley's ranch. They'd be able to search the premises for Rachel and the others before dealing with him. Once they encountered him, he'd know this was the end of the road for him. She didn't expect him to go down easy.

She got out of her car to open the rickety gate.

She smelled smoke before she saw the black furls sweeping above the treetops. It could be just a trash fire.

It could be Roy Sales's last hurrah.

Panic jolted her into action. The latch on the gate was locked. She ran back to the car and barged through the gate, knocking one side completely off its rusty hinges.

Her plan to wait for Jackson to arrive was canceled. She followed the smoke until she was close enough to see brilliant gold and yellow blazes shooting toward the sky.

By the time she reached what was left of the house, timbers were falling and most of the roof was gone.

She jumped out of her car and heard women screaming for help, their voices almost drowned out completely by the roar of the flames.

"I'm coming, Rachel. I'm coming," she screamed. She rushed toward the fire. The heat and smoke stole her breath but she kept pushing on.

Her eyes poured water. Her lungs burned. Coughing spells tore from her dry throat. The fiery blazes were lapping at everything around her. Struggling to stay conscious, she fell to her knees. Then she looked up and saw three women stumbling hand in hand from the blaze. Coughing and fighting for breath, they fell to the ground in a huddle the second they were out of harm's way.

Sydney crawled toward them, her heart beating so fast it pushed her along. Finally, she escaped the worst of the fire and called out for Rachel.

The women turned toward her. None of the three were Rachel. Dizzy and nauseous, Sydney stumbled back toward the flames. She could swear she heard Rachel calling her name. She fell to her knees as the heat overtook her.

She tried to get up, but her legs wouldn't move. She was so hot, so very, very hot. Someone picked her up in his arms as a huge timber crashed around her. Or maybe it was death calling her home.

Blinded by smoke and tears, she looked up and had to blink repeatedly before she realized it was Tucker who had saved her from the flames.

"How did you get here? Where did you come from?"

"Jackson called and said you were here waiting on backup."

"I didn't save Rachel."

"I know. I'm so sorry, baby. So very sorry. God knows you tried."

Reality merged with grief. She wiggled out of his arms but held to Tucker to keep her balance even after her feet were planted on solid ground. "We have to help the women who just escaped that literal hell."

When she turned to find them, they were no longer there.

"There were three women who walked out of the fire. I didn't dream them, did I?"

"The only person I saw was you," Tucker said.

"I know they were here. Everyone except Rachel was right here a few minutes ago. The fire must have burned the locked doors that held them."

"Jackson's on his way here. If they're here, he'll find them. Let's get you to my truck."

"I'm not leaving here until we find them." She rushed off into the woods to look for them.

"Sydney, over here."

The voice was the quietest of whispers but Sydney was certain it was Rachel calling to her. Rachel. Alive.

"I'm coming," she called through sobs of

pure joy and thankful release. “Oh, Rachel, I’m coming.”

Finally, she caught a glimpse of her sister motioning to her from behind a thick tree trunk.

Moving as quickly as she could, she made her way to Rachel. She collapsed into Rachel’s arms, holding on tight, afraid to believe Rachel was really alive and safe.

“Don’t make a sound,” Rachel whispered. “The monster is out there somewhere, Sydney. He’s always there.”

“No, you’re safe,” Sydney whispered. Safe. Her sister was safe and alive. Relief surged through her as she let the feeling sink deep into her heart.

“My friend Tucker is waiting for us. The FBI is on the way. The monster is history.”

“No. You’ll see. He’s never going to let me go. He’ll kill us both.”

“Why do you think that?”

“Because he always does what he says.”

This time the voice was gruff and Sydney felt the barrel of a gun pressed against her temple. Rachel was right. The monster had been there all along.

“So this is the way you want it, Rachel?

You'd rather run away from me and burn to death than stay with me. In that case, who wants to die first? Oh, that's right. I promised Rachel she could watch her sister die. Or was it the other way around?"

Sydney took a deep breath. She'd been here before. That time the Strangler had the upper hand. This time it was the Lone Star Snatcher, but the situation was the same.

Take control or die. If she was going to die anyway, what did she have to lose?

The gun was at her head. A quick pull of the trigger and it would all be over and the Snatcher would win. She and Rachel would be the monster's last victims.

She was not ready to die. She had a bull rider waiting for her and a whole marvelous life to live.

She tripped intentionally and fell backward, maneuvering her body so she'd fall against Roy Sales's injured leg. Roy yelled out in pain and then raised his pistol to slam it into her head.

Instead it went flying through the woods.

"Sorry, Roy. Not my first rodeo and you just bought yourself lifetime accommodations in the state pen. Now, would one of you ladies mind picking up Roy's gun and handing it to me? I hated to get it dirty but he wasn't playing nice with it."

"Tucker." Sydney turned to find the situation reversed. Tucker was a step behind Roy with his gun pointed at Roy's head.

No one had ever looked that good to her in all her life.

A symphony of sirens signaled the approach of the sheriff, Jackson and hopefully a fire truck or two.

Alice, Michelle and Karen joined them at the edge of the woods. All the women ended up crying thankful tears in each other's arms.

Each of the women would go back to their lives a different person than they were before this horrible experience, but they were going back alive. Sydney would be there to help Rachel through her adjustment every step of the way.

The reign of the Lone Star Snatcher was over, but that wouldn't end the evil in this world. That was why Sydney would be staying with the FBI. Somebody had to fight for right. She loved the job, so it might as well be her.

Unless that meant giving up Tucker. In

which case she might have to reexamine her whole life to this point.

Rachel and Sydney met briefly with Jackson. A more detailed meeting was set for first thing the following morning, after both of them had some rest and recovery time.

Rachel went back to Esther's with Sydney and Tucker, and his marvelous family welcomed her with warm, embracing arms.

It was hours later before Sydney and Tucker finally made it to her bed. This time Tucker got to stay all night and they finally made love.

Three times.

Epilogue

Three weeks later:

Tucker had returned to the rodeo. He loved it as much as ever and was thankful he hadn't walked away from it. But rodeo wasn't all he loved.

He was head over heels crazy about Sydney but the relationship seemed to be stalling out at the commitment stage. He'd always heard it was men who were afraid of commitment, but he couldn't wait to promise forever. Sydney wouldn't even mention the *c* word.

The ring was in his pocket, but what would he do if she said no? Beg? Not his style.

Riding bulls had never been this scary. He walked out to the porch to wait for Sydney. She was driving in from Dallas, where she said she had an important meeting with Jackson today.

He'd driven in from Waco, where he'd just come in first in the bull-riding competition.

He and Sydney had to do a lot of planning to get time together, but it was always worth the trouble. Not just making love with her, as fantastic and exciting as that was. He loved every second he spent with her.

Esther joined him, a glass of tea in hand. She sat down in her porch swing and watched him pace.

"What's gotten into you tonight? You're as wired as an electric line."

"I'm just looking forward to seeing Sydney."

"You two aren't having problems, are you?"

"Not that I know of."

"Don't you mess it up with her, Tucker. She's smart, sweet and fun. You're not going to run into many women like that in a lifetime of looking."

"I agree."

"I sure do appreciate her getting me some closure on my Charlie's death. I knew he didn't commit suicide. We loved each other too much for him to just check out on me like that. It didn't make me miss him any less, but all the same it was salve for my grief."

"Good to finally get justice for Charlie," Tucker said. "I'm not surprised to find out Millie was behind the killing or that Roy Sales could be lured into the murderous scheme with her money. I am shocked Millie finally admitted her part in that. She'll be behind bars for a long, long time."

"My Charlie was just so honest," Esther said. "He knew his friend Dudley wasn't guilty and that Millie was always letting Angela get by with anything. When Charlie went to her and threatened to tell the truth, she just up and had him killed."

"Charlie is just another trial Roy Sales will be facing. He also confessed to the murder of Sara Goodwin."

"Do they have any idea why he killed her?" Esther asked.

"The theory that's being tossed around is her murder is what triggered his going over the edge. He thought she wanted to be with him and then she started calling him the same sort of names his mother used to call him."

"The dark-haired mother who looked a lot like Rachel and his other victims," Esther said.

"They say his mother used to lock him up in the basement for days if he just spilled his milk or got his clothes dirty playing outside. What kind of momma would do a thing like that?"

"One that shouldn't have had children," Tucker said. "Sales had his problems. That didn't give him the right to kill and torture others."

"What he done was bad and that's for sure," Esther said. "But even though he killed Charlie, I'm glad they put him in that mental hospital to see if he's fit to stand trial. The psychologist said Roy Sales even believed he'd killed his mother because he wished she was dead when she tortured him. Truth was she just accidentally fell from a ladder."

"I suppose the defense will claim the torture he went through as a child was what caused him to lock Rachel and the others up in that crowded storm shelter," Tucker said. "Too bad he didn't get help before he caused so much hurt to so many people."

A car pulled up in front of the house and stopped. When Sydney stepped out, Tucker hurried to meet her.

She fell into his open arms and they stayed that way for long minutes.

"How did your meeting go?" he asked.

"Great. I can't wait to tell you about it."

"Then don't." He opened the trunk to get her luggage. "Let's hear it."

"It's not something I want to just blurt out."

He wasn't sure he was going to like this. "Want to take a walk before we go inside?"

"I do."

This was starting to sound like a breakup moment. He stuck his hand deep in his pocket and worried the engagement ring he'd hoped to put on her finger tonight.

They walked awhile in silence before Sydney broke her news. "I've been offered a really nice promotion but it will require moving to Dallas."

"Are you going to take it?"

"That all depends on you."

"I'm not sure what you mean."

"I love you, Tucker. I love you so much that I can't even imagine living without you. But I love my job, too. And you love bull riding. Living in Texas instead of Nashville would make it easier for us to get together, but I'm still not sure we would ever have enough time for us."

"We'll make time. It will take effort but we can do it. Vacations. Days I'm not in competition, I'll spend with you. Weekends you can fly to meet me wherever I'm competing."

"Will you settle for that?"

"I guess the real question is, will either of us settle for less? We don't fit into the one-size-fits-all mold, Sydney. We take risks. We go for the passion, at least that's what a wise woman once told me."

"What if she was wrong?"

"I know her well. She meant every word of it and she's almost never wrong. As brave as you are, don't tell me you're afraid to take a chance on us."

He curled his fingers around the ring in his pocket and then fell to one knee.

"I love you, Sydney Maxwell. I have since the first day I met you. I don't want you to give up something you love for me. That would only diminish both of us."

"And you can be happy with my continuing to work for the FBI?" she asked.

"I certainly can't be happy if you're not happy. We'll go through lots of changes in our life. My body definitely won't hold up to bull riding forever. You might want a family one day. But we'll change on our terms when we're good and ready."

He took her hand. "Will you marry me and join me in the best damn love affair in the history of all mankind? All it has to last is forever."

"You're sure."

"I've never been more sure of anything in my life."

"Then the answer is yes. I love you, Tucker, and I have no doubts that marriage to you will be the most exciting adventure of my life."

He slipped the ring on her finger, stood and took her in his arms. They sealed their promises with a kiss that took his breath away.

A thrill a minute with Sydney for as long as they lived. It couldn't get any better than that.

* * * * *